TEXAS REBELS: EGAN

BY
LINDA WARREN

MILLS & BOON

Published in Great Britain 2015
by Mills & Boon, an imprint of Harlequin (UK) Limited,
Eton House, 18-24 Paradise Road, Richmond, Surrey, TW9 1SR

© 2015 Linda Warren

ISBN: 978-0-263-25131-9

23-0415

Harlequin (UK) Limited's policy is to use papers that are natural, renewable and recyclable products and made from wood grown in sustainable forests. The logging and manufacturing processes conform to the legal environmental regulations of the country of origin.

Printed and bound in Spain
by CPI, Barcelona

Two-time RITA® Award-nominated and award-winning author **Linda Warren** loves her job, writing happily-ever-after books for Mills & Boon. Drawing upon her years of growing up on a farm/ranch in Texas, she writes about sexy heroes, feisty heroines and broken families with an emotional punch, all set against the backdrop of Texas. Her favorite pastime is sitting on her patio with her husband watching the wildlife, especially the injured ones that are coming in pairs these days: two Canada geese with broken wings, two does with broken legs and a bobcat ready to pounce on anything tasty. Learn more about Linda and her books at her website, lindawarren. net, or on Facebook, LindaWarrenAuthor, or follow @ Texauthor on Twitter.

I dedicate this book to Helen Sheffield, friend, author, teacher and supporter of anyone who was interested in writing. She encouraged and supported me over the years and I'm grateful for having known her. She was an amazing, loving, giving person who never met a stranger. Rest in peace, my friend.

Acknowledgements

A big thank-you to the internet. The research for this book was done solely online: weeks of researching and double-checking and chatting to people who were nice enough to share their knowledge, especially about dog bites, prison and court proceedings.

Prologue

My name is Kate Rebel. I married John Rebel when I
was eighteen years old and then bore him seven sons.
We worked the family ranch, which John later inher-
ited. We put everything we had into buying more land
so our sons would have a legacy. We didn't have much,
but we had love.

The McCray Ranch borders Rebel Ranch on the east
and the McCrays have forever been a thorn in my family's side. They've cut our fences, dammed up creeks to
limit our water supply and shot one of our prize bulls.
Ezra McCray threatened to shoot our sons if he caught
them jumping his fences again. We tried to keep our boys
away, but they are boys—young and wild.

One day Jude and Phoenix, two of our youngest, were
out riding together. When John heard shots, he immediately went to find his boys. They lay on the ground,
blood oozing from their heads. Ezra McCray was astride
a horse twenty yards away with a rifle in his hand. John
drew his gun and fired, killing Ezra instantly. Both boys
survived with only minor wounds. Since my husband was
protecting his children, he didn't spend even one night
in jail. This escalated the feud that still goes on today.

The man I knew as my husband died that day. He
couldn't live with what he'd done, and started to drink

heavily. I had to take over the ranch and the raising of our boys. John died ten years later. We've all been affected by the tragedy, especially my sons.

They are grown men now and deal in different ways with the pain of losing their father. One day I pray my boys will be able to put this behind them and live healthy, normal lives with women who will love them the way I loved their father.

Chapter One

Egan: the third son—the loner

A cowboy's work was never done.

Holidays, weekends, in bitter cold and extreme heat, Egan Rebel was in the saddle on Rebel Ranch, herding cattle, branding, tagging, vaccinating, fixing fences and feeding. It never ended. But that's who he was—a cowboy. It was a whole lot better than staring at cell bars in front of his face.

Freedom was free, or so they said, but for Egan it came with a price. One he paid every day of his life. He meandered his horse through a herd of red-and-white cattle, forcing the thoughts away. His dog, Pete, trailed behind, on watch in case a moody cow decided to charge.

The vast Texas ranch stretched across miles and miles of gently rolling hills dotted with oak, elm, yaupon, cedar and mesquite, then down into lush valleys of coastal hay fields, prairies of wildflowers and woods so thick only daylight could squeeze through. Two creeks and various natural springs flowed on the property. No place on earth could compare to the spectacular sunrises or the awe-inspiring sunsets. This was paradise on earth to Egan. Fresh air, blue skies and freedom. He'd left here once to his peril, but he would never leave again.

Buzzards circled overhead. He pulled up. A cow bellowed in distress at the edge of the woods. He kneed his horse, Gypsy, in that direction. When he saw the problem he swung from the saddle, the leather creaking as he did. A baby calf lay dead in the grass.

Jericho Johnson rode in and surveyed the scene. "What happened?" Jericho was Egan's best friend. He'd saved Egan's life in prison and for that Egan would always be grateful. Egan's mother, Kate, had given Jericho a job and a home for his actions. They didn't know much about the man, but Egan knew what was important.

He squatted by the red-and-white calf and pointed. "Teeth marks around its neck. A fun kill. Probably by a pack of feral dogs or wolves. This makes the eighth calf this month."

Pete sniffed the ground and barked.

Egan followed the dog into the woods. "Come back, boy," he called, and Pete trotted to his side.

"There are tracks leading to the McCray property." Egan walked toward his horse. "The woods are too thick for a horse. Take the horses and Pete back to the ranch. I'm going to keep tracking on foot."

Jericho removed his hat and scratched his head. He was a big man, about six-four. His nationality was unknown, but he'd once told Egan he was a little bit white, Mexican, Indian and black. With his long hair and a scar slashed down the side of his face, he was known to scare the strongest of men.

"Do you think that's wise?"

Jericho knew of the feud with the McCrays and that avoiding them was always the best policy.

Egan removed his rifle from the saddle scabbard. "Crazy Isadore McCray has dogs and I just want to see if they've crossed over onto Rebel land. If Izzy has been killing our calves, I'll call the sheriff. I don't plan on being stupid and confronting him. Stupid once in a life-time is all I can handle."

"If the two of us track—"

Egan cut him off with a dark stare. "I know these woods like the back of my hand and I don't need any help tracking. Tell Mom and Falcon I'm on it."

Jericho inclined his head. "You got it." He reached for the reins of Egan's horse. "But if you're not at the ranch by tomorrow, I'll come looking."

Egan nodded to his friend and squatted in front of Pete. "Go back to the ranch with Rico." He rubbed the dog's head. He didn't want the feral dogs to kill him. Pete was an Australian blue healer, a cow dog, but if it came to a fight, he would be right in the middle of it.

Tipping his hat, Jericho rode away, Pete trotting be-hind. The dog stopped once to look back, but Egan didn't motion for him to come, so he continued his journey be-hind the horses.

Egan shoved his hand into the pocket of his dark duster and pulled out his phone. No signal. He was alone, but it had been that way most of his life, even with six brothers.

Following the trail into the woods, he pushed through yaupons and mesquite. He kept his eyes focused on the ground. From the tracks, there had to be at least six dogs and one man. The woods grew thicker and the tracks dis-appeared, almost into thin air. He was close enough to the McCray property line to know Izzy had been up to no good. Egan may have told Rico he wouldn't do any-thing stupid, but he wasn't about to let Izzy kill any more calves on Rebel Ranch.

RACHEL HOLLISTER WAS LOST.

For over an hour, she'd been traveling this country back road and the scenery had changed from mesquite and scrub to thick woods. She cursed herself for being a coward and taking the long way home. She'd been away twelve years and still she was stalling, avoiding the moment she would walk in the door of the home she'd shared with her mother and family. The mother who had died because of her. Twelve years was long enough to deal with the guilt. The grief. Or maybe not. It was part of her now.

Every morning when she looked in the mirror she saw herself, but she also saw a young girl who'd been spoiled, pampered and far too used to getting her own way. Rachel didn't like that girl and had had years to change her. But she hadn't changed enough to face the past. That was evident by her taking this cutoff to nowhere. If she'd stayed on US 77 she would already be in Horseshoe.

She'd left the blacktop some time ago and now the road narrowed to merely a track. Her heart lifted when she saw a cattle guard. There had to be a house somewhere and she could ask for directions. She looked around for signs of human life, a barn, anything. But all she saw were woods and more woods. The track ended and she had nowhere to go.

Just then the engine made a funny sound and she could barely turn the steering wheel. She stopped and listened. The motor was still running but the car wouldn't go. Now what?

She reached for her phone in her purse and tried to call her brother. No signal. She looked out the window and couldn't see power lines. Where was she? Rachel got out of the car and an eerie feeling came over her. The May wind rustled through the trees, the only sound she heard.

She tried her phone again. Nothing. A sliver of alarm shot through her and she got back into the car. How was she going to get out of here? She mustn't panic. She shut off the engine and waited ten minutes. When she started it again it sounded strange, not like before. She put the car in gear and pressed the gas. The steering wheel was still hard to turn and she knew she couldn't go very far like this. She turned off the ignition.

Her choices were simple. She'd have to walk out or sit here and wait for someone to find her. From the silence, she feared that wait might be long. A tear slipped from her eye and she slapped it away. She could handle this.

She got out of the car again and looked down at her dress and heels. Not ideal for walking. Her suitcase was in the backseat, so she'd just change into jeans and sneakers.

As Rachel moved toward the door, something in her peripheral vision caught her eye. Her heart thumped against her chest. There was a man emerging from the woods. He was hard to see because he seemed as one with his surroundings. A dark duster like she'd seen cowboys wear in olden days flapped around his legs. His longish dark hair brushed against his collar, and he had at least a day's worth of stubble. A worn hat was pulled low over his eyes, but what held her attention was the rifle in his hand.

Fear crept along her nerves as she got back into the car, locking the doors manually. The man continued to stride toward her. There was nothing she could do but wait. Who was he? And what was he doing out here so far from anywhere?

Her eyes were glued to him as he drew closer. She scooted away from the window, as if that would help. When he tapped on the window, she jumped; she was so nervous.

"Are you okay, ma'am?"

He peered at her through the window and she stared into the darkest eyes she'd ever seen. Instead of being paralyzed with fear, her body relaxed. His eyes were riveting. It was like coming in from an icy cold day into a room with a roaring fire. All she felt was the warmth, and she instinctively knew this man wouldn't hurt her.

"Ma'am, are you okay?" he repeated, and his strong voice propelled her into action. She turned on the motor and reached for the window button, but nothing happened. The window wouldn't move. She had no choice but to open the door.

As she got out, he stepped back and she realized he was tall. Even in her heels she had to look up.

"What are you doing out here?" His voice was deep, masculine and irritated.

"I'm lost," she admitted. "I was headed to Horseshoe."

"You're miles away from Horseshoe."

She knew that. "I was hoping to find a house and get directions, but there don't seem to be any homes nearby."

"No." He pointed. "Across that fence line is the McCray property and you're standing on Rebel Ranch. The cattle guard is a back entrance in case we need it. If you turn around and follow the track, it will lead you to a road. You should be able to find your way then."

"That's the problem. Something's wrong with my car. It started making funny noises and now I can't turn the steering wheel. And the windows won't work, either." She looked into those beautiful eyes. "Do you know anything about cars?"

He placed his rifle against the vehicle. "Unlatch the hood and I'll take a look."

Unlatch the hood? "Uh…" She had no idea what he was talking about, and it was no use pretending that she did. "This is a rental and I don't know anything about cars."

He didn't roll his eyes or anything like that. He just

reached inside her car and pulled something. A pop sounded. He walked to the front of the car and with both hands lifted the hood. Peering over, she watched as he looked around.

He finally straightened. "Your serpentine belt is broken. It controls a lot of the extras on your car, like power steering, power windows and AC. I'm not sure about this model, but it can also control the water pump, which means driving could be dangerous." He slammed the hood shut.

"Do you live nearby?" she asked with a hopeful note.

"Miles away. I'm out tracking feral dogs."

"What?" Had she heard him correctly? She had this eerie feeling she'd stepped back into the 1800s.

"Dogs are killing our calves on the ranch." When he sensed she wasn't following him, he waved his hand. "You can just follow the track to the road. It'll take you an hour or so, but someone will eventually find you."

She looked down at her heels.

"Do you have other shoes?" That note of irritation was back in his voice.

"In my suitcase."

"My suggestion is you change and start moving, because it's going to be dark soon."

The thought of walking alone at night filled her with a claustrophobic feeling. "I really don't want to walk alone. I'll pay you if you help me get to Horseshoe."

He sighed. "Ma'am, I don't need your money. I just need to get back to doing my job before any more calves die on the ranch."

"You can't just leave me out here. I know there are wild animals and no telling what else. It's dangerous."

"And that didn't cross your mind when you were traveling miles and miles without a sign of life?"

"I was looking for Cutoff 149."

"They changed that many years ago. The roads now have county numbers so it's easier for emergency vehicles and firefighters."

"It's been a long time since I've been to Horseshoe."

"Then why not stay on 77?"

He was annoyed and he was making *her* annoyed. She placed her hands on her hips. "Are you going to help me or not?"

He glanced off to the woods and then at her. "Looks like I don't have any choice, and I lost the tracks a while ago. If we walk directly east, it should take about two hours to reach a spot where we can get cell phone reception. Then I can call the ranch and someone can meet us in an all-terrain vehicle. Change clothes. I'll give you a few minutes." He strolled away without a backward glance.

Goose bumps popped up on her skin. He wouldn't leave her here, would he? Her gut instinct said no. She didn't know anything about him, but she sensed he was a man she could trust. Climbing into the backseat, she took a long breath and did a quick change. She felt like Houdini.

This was all her fault and she was angry at herself. She was glad she hadn't called her father or her brother to let them know she was coming home. They would be worried sick when she didn't show up. Now they were really going to be surprised. How could one day go so wrong?

EGAN GAVE THE woman a few minutes, wondering how he'd gotten himself into this mess. He didn't have time to fool with some ditzy blonde. Being judgmental wasn't part of his nature, so he should give the woman the benefit of the doubt. But she was far from civilization and it was going to take a big chunk out of his workday to help her. It all depended on how fast she could walk. If he had to guess, he would say it was going to be a slow go.

When he returned to the car, she was standing outside. He took one look and wondered if this woman had any sense at all. She wore short jeans. They had a name, but for the life of him he couldn't think of it. She had a pink-and-white layered top and pink-and-white sneakers.

He motioned toward the jeans. "Do you have longer ones?"

"No. It's spring so I brought spring and summer clothes. These are capris."

"And unsuitable for hiking through the woods."

Her face crumpled like a little kid's and he thought she was going to cry. "It's all I have besides shorts and another dress."

"It will have to do. Do you have a long-sleeved blouse or a sweater? It'll get chilly in these hills as it grows darker."

"I have a lime-green lightweight sweater that goes with my dress, but it doesn't match what I have on."

He laughed. He couldn't help himself. He'd gotten himself involved with a city diva.

Her face broke into a smile. "That was silly."

"Yes, it was. We're not going to a party. We'll be hiking through rough terrain and trying to avoid every pesky critter we can. There will be thick woods, brambles, snakes, bugs and every animal from field mice to whitetail deer to bobcats. And believe me, they won't care what you're wearing."

"I assure you I'm not a weak woman. I can handle this."

"You'll pardon me if I don't quite believe that. You're a city girl."

She lifted her chin with determination. "I'm a city woman and I'm stronger than I look."

"Well, city woman, let's go. Just follow me and don't complain and don't ask questions."

"Wait." She grabbed her purse and the sweater from the car. She tied the sweater around her neck and slung the purse over her shoulder. Then she got in line behind him as if they were going on a march or something. He shook his head and started off.

For the first thirty minutes she followed on his heels, but the longer they walked, the farther she trailed behind. She was getting tired and wouldn't admit it, so he slowed down to give her a break. The problem was, they wouldn't make it far enough to get cell reception before dark.

The woods were beautiful this time of year. The browns of fall and winter had turned to lively shades of green. New life. New season. New beginnings. Rabbits and squirrels scurried about and birds chirped in perfect harmony, the best music to guide their way. A snake slithered up a tree, but he didn't show her. He feared she might freak out. He glanced back to check how far behind she was, and saw the sun setting in the west. Without thinking, he pointed.

She gasped as she viewed the beautiful oranges and reds that emanated from the large, fiery ball. "How beautiful. It looks as if the woods are on fire."

He never grew tired of watching the sun set in Texas on Rebel Ranch. It made him aware that there were more important things in the world than his tiny problems.

"We might as well bed down for the night."

She stared at him with something close to shock in her eyes. "Out here? Maybe our cells will work now."

"They won't. We didn't make it far enough."

She reached in her purse and pulled out her phone.

After several attempts to call, she gave up. "Can we keep walking?"

"It's too dangerous at night. We'll stay here and start again in the morning."

"I went camping once when I was a kid, and I didn't like it. I don't think I'm going to like it now, either."

He laid his rifle on the ground and removed his duster. He spread it out on the sparse grass. "We can rest on this."

Without a word she sank onto it. Her breathing was labored. "I don't mean to complain or anything, but water would be heavenly."

"I was thinking the same thing." He knelt and fished a canteen from the pocket of the duster.

"What's that?"

"It's a collapsible canteen. See—" he unfolded the durable plastic "—we have something to drink out of."

"But we have no water."

"There's a natural spring not far from here."

She got up on her knees. "You're not going to leave me here?"

"I won't be far. Just holler if something happens."

She sank back on the duster as if in defeat. He watched her for a moment and thought she was holding up well for a city woman.

It didn't take him long to find the spring. He filled the canteen and drank from it, and then filled it again for her. When he returned, she was sitting on the duster with her arms wrapped around her waist, watching the woods warily. It was getting dark now and her eyes lit up at the sight him. He realized for the first time they were blue—a brilliant, beautiful blue, like a field of Texas bluebonnets.

He sat beside her as she drank the water.

"This is divine."

"It's springwater and the best there is."

She handed him the canteen and he shook his head. "I drank at the spring."

"Wait." She dug around in her purse and pulled out two chocolate bars. "I forgot I have Kit Kat bars. I never go anywhere without chocolate."

"No, tha—"

She held one in front of his face. "Eat it. It's all we have."

Before he knew it, he was eating a candy bar with her.

The darkness closed in like a wall, isolating them. It was a dark night and they couldn't see beyond their hands as crickets serenaded them. The quarter moon hung like a big, bright banana and served as a small spotlight of reassurance that the world was still out there.

She scooted back on the duster. "Thank you for doing this."

"Yeah." What else did she want him to say?

"I don't think we introduced ourselves. You said you worked on Rebel Ranch. Do you know the Rebel family?"

"You could say that. I'm Egan Rebel."

"Oh, are you Phoenix's brother?"

"Yes." It felt a little strange that she knew his family.

"He was in my class in school. He spiked the punch at one of my parties and got everyone drunk."

"That's Phoenix. The life of the party."

"He was always fun to be around, but he was one of the wild boys the girls were told to stay away from. All the Rebel boys were known for that, but it didn't keep the girls from talking about them or wanting to go out with them."

"Did you want to go out with Phoenix?"

"No. He really was a little wild for me. I was timid in school."

"That's hard to believe."

"It was twelve years ago. I've matured and now wild boys don't scare me at all." She scooted forward. "I'm Rachel…Rachel Hollister."

Egan's chest caved in. It took a moment before he could speak. She couldn't be… No way. But he had to ask the question. "Are you Judge Hollister's daughter?"

"Yes. Do you know my father?"

Egan was a mild-mannered man and hate didn't come easily for him, but he hated Judge Hollister. The man had sent him to prison without any hard evidence. He'd sent him into the bowels of hell and Egan had barely escaped with his life. It seemed surreal that he was sitting here with his daughter. A daughter the man loved. For a brief moment he wondered how Judge Hollister would feel if he lost his daughter. Egan wanted him to feel some of the pain he'd felt.

Could he be the criminal Judge Hollister had branded him?

Chapter Two

"I can't sleep." The woman twisted and turned.

"Just be still."

"I'm trying, but the ground is so hard." She sat up and untied the sweater from around her neck. Wadding it into a ball, she placed it on the duster and used it for a pillow. "That's better."

After a few minutes she grew still and Egan knew she was close to sleep. The temperature had dropped for the evening and it was cooler. She curled into a ball with her arms wrapped around her waist. He reached over, grabbed the end of the duster and pulled it over her legs so she wouldn't be cold. When he did that, he knew he couldn't harm one hair on her head. He wasn't that type of man. No matter what Judge Hollister had done to him, he had no desire for revenge. At least, not that type of revenge.

"What time do you think it is?" she asked, surprising him.

"I thought you were asleep."

"No. I'm just tired."

"Rest, then."

"Aren't you going to sleep?"

"In a minute."

She sat up. "It's so dark and quiet, except for the crickets. It's like I'm having a bad dream."

Egan wrapped his arms around his knees. "Yeah." If he closed his eyes, he could hear the shouts, the filthy cuss words, the goading and the ugly faces of evil. He'd thought he was tough, but he didn't know tough until he had to stand toe-to-toe with hardened criminals.

"I feel so stupid," she murmured.

"Why?" Her words brought him back from the abyss that always threatened to take him down.

"Because I'm a coward. I should have stayed on US 77 and I'd be home now, facing my past the way I was supposed to. The way I'd planned."

"You have a past?" He couldn't imagine what kind of a dire past a beautiful blonde could have.

"My parents spoiled me terribly."

"Pardon me, but I don't consider that a past."

"If you'll listen, I'll tell you," she snapped.

"Yes, ma'am."

"I love the way you say ma'am."

"I say it like everybody else in Texas."

"No, you say it with respect and I feel it."

That threw him, so he just sat and stared at the blanket of twinkling stars and waited for her to speak.

"My mother was killed when I was seventeen."

"I remember that. She was shot by gang members while walking to her car in a mall, right?"

"Yes. She was in the wrong place at the wrong time… all because of me."

He knew he should stop with the questions. He didn't want to get any more involved with her than he already was. But something in her voice prompted him to ask, "What did you have to do with it?"

She didn't answer and the silence stretched. They kept

looking at the beautiful night sky above them. Then her voice came, low and achy. "I haven't told anyone this and I don't know why I'm telling you. I just need to say the words—to hear them out loud." She paused. "It happened on a Friday. There was a dance at my school on Saturday and I wanted this special dress that I'd seen. I begged and begged my mother to buy it, and she said no, that I had plenty of dresses." A muffled sound followed the words and he knew Rachel was crying. He remained still, not making any movement because he had a feeling she didn't want him to react. And he wasn't comfortable with that type of emotion.

"She must've changed her mind because that's what she was doing at the mall—buying my dress. The police gave it to me later and I threw it in the garbage. I killed...my mother."

"Come on, you can't possibly believe that."

"She wouldn't have been at that mall if I hadn't continually kept asking for the dress."

"But it was her choice to go."

Rachel rested her chin on her knees. "My mother was the most loving person I've ever known, and she didn't deserve to die like that. I just can't forget it and I've tried. For twelve years I've been trying. I went to art school in Paris, hoping that would obliterate the guilt, but it didn't. I longed for home and my mother. But she wasn't there anymore."

"I don't know anything about your mother, but I'm almost positive she wouldn't want you to live with the guilt."

"I tell myself that all the time and it doesn't make that ache go away."

"Have you talked to someone in your family?"

The answer was a long time coming. "No. I wanted

to tell my best friend, Angie, and my brother, but I could never find the right words."

Egan stared into the darkness and tried to find words of his own to help her. That blew his mind, because he didn't want to help her. But there was something about her that just begged for protection. His mama had always told him he could never resist a person in need. Even when he considered them the enemy.

"You don't have a past. You have a guilt complex, and the only way to get rid of it is to talk to your family, the ones who are close to you." Judge Hollister's name stuck in his craw and he couldn't say it out loud.

"That's what I finally decided to do. You probably know that my brother, Hardy, married Angie Wiznowski, and they have a new baby. I'm dying to see him and to meet their older daughter, Erin, so I planned to come home and deal with all the guilt. And what did I do?" She slapped the top of her knee with her right hand. "At the last minute, I balked and stalled for time by taking the long way and getting lost. Now here I sit with a very nice stranger, wondering if maybe I'm losing my mind."

"You're not. Tomorrow we'll make it to the ranch and you can call your family and talk and tell them how you're feeling. I'm told talking works wonders."

"Mmm. You don't like to talk, do you?"

"Nope. It's not my favorite thing."

"Are you married?"

They were getting into personal territory and he certainly didn't like that. Talking about himself was his least favorite subject. A coyote howled in the distance, diverting her attention.

"How close is that?" she asked, edging a little nearer to him.

"Not very."

"You didn't answer my question. Are you married?"

He gritted his teeth. She was one of those women who just wouldn't let go. "No. I'm not married. If I was, I wouldn't be spending the night in these woods."

"Have you ever been married?"

"Ma'am, it's time to get some rest."

"Since you said that so nicely, I will." She wrapped her arms around herself "It's getting chilly."

"You can use the duster. It'll keep you warm."

"I will not." She shoved her right arm into a sleeve. "Now, do the same with your left."

"What…"

"Remember, you said no complaining."

He shoved his arm into the hole and it drew them together inside the duster. Maybe too close together. A flowery scent from her hair reached his nostrils, and he wanted to pull away, but there was nowhere to go.

"See, this way we both can stay warm," she said, with a smile in her voice. "Now we just lie back and go to sleep."

He grunted, but did as she'd instructed. It took a moment for them to get comfortable. They tried several positions, and finally, lying on their sides worked best. Her soft curves fitted nicely into his hardened body. It had been a long time since he'd been with a woman and the feeling was doing a familiar number on his senses. All he had to do was remember who she was and his mind cleared. For a second.

"Are you going to sleep with your hat on?"

"Is that a problem?"

"No." She wiggled against him and that *was* a problem. "I just find it strange."

"I spent a lot of time in these woods, and on one occasion I took off my hat and the next morning it was gone. A varmint had stolen it. A raccoon is probably wearing it now."

"I like you, Egan Rebel."

Don't like me. Please don't like me!

"Go to sleep."

"Call me ma'am."

"Go to sleep."

"I will if…"

"Go to sleep…ma'am."

She laughed, a tingly sound that warmed parts of his heart that had been cold for a long time. He immediately shut out the sound and the feeling.

After a moment, he heard her easy breathing and knew she had fallen asleep. It was a long time before he could succumb to the tiredness of his mind and his body. He had to have the most rotten luck in the world. How ironic was it that he would rescue the judge-from-hell's daughter? His beautiful daughter.

This had to be one of the worst days of Egan's life.

RACHEL WOKE UP to aches and pains, yet felt oddly relaxed. She turned her head and found Egan staring at her with those beautiful eyes. A masculine, woodsy scent reached her and her stomach curled into a pleasant knot. With his hat still on his head, he gave ruggedly handsome a new meaning. The lines of his face were pronounced, his growth of beard arousing, his nose straight and his mouth a sexy slash, begging to be touched and experienced. She licked her lips, wanting that pleasure.

"You're awake," he said.

"Yeah," she murmured.

He already had his arm out of the duster and now sat up. She felt a bereavement she couldn't explain. She wondered what he would say if she invited him to touch her, to hold her, to… What was wrong with her? Her mind was straying into dangerous territory. She wasn't that type of woman. But looking at Egan Rebel, she wanted to be.

With one swift movement, he was on his feet. She, on the other hand, was a little slower. Dawn was breaking over the valley below and she stood for a moment to gaze at the beauty of God's creation. It was as if God had kissed the night into submission and now the sun could show its glory. It did, in beautiful rays of yellow, a breathtaking scene. She wished she had a canvas to paint it, but she would keep it in her memory for later. Just as she would the man standing beside her.

"I'm going to get some water," he said.

She reached for her purse and pulled out a small sketch pad she kept.

"What are you doing?"

"I want to sketch this scene so I can paint it later."

Egan shook his head and disappeared into the woods.

Rachel sat cross-legged with the sketch pad on her lap. She drew broad strokes. The scene before her faded and Egan's face appeared. The strong lines, longish hair, hat, the shape of his eyes and that steadfast, masculine demeanor. It was all there with each stroke. She stared at it for a moment and then tucked the pad back into her purse. No matter what happened, she would have a memory of this unforgettable man.

Seeing her hairbrush in the purse, she pulled it out and attempted to work the tangles from her hair. A sound caught her attention and she turned her head. She froze. Fear leaped into her throat. Wild-looking dogs stood near the edge of the woods, baring their teeth and growling. A bearded man stood behind them with a rifle.

Rachel tried to get to her feet, but her shaky legs

wouldn't comply. Before she could process the situation, the man said something to the dogs and they charged toward her.

Oh my God!

She scrambled to her feet, trying to run, but the dogs were upon her. "Egan! Egan!" she screamed.

EGAN DROPPED THE canteen and ran, the rifle in his hand. The scene before him chilled his blood. A dog was on Rachel, ferociously trying to reach her throat. She beat at it with a hairbrush, foiling its attempts. Two more dogs tore at her clothes. Another joined the attack. Rachel kicked and screamed, the sound disrupting the peace and quiet with spine-tingling terror.

He raised his rifle and fired. One dog went down. He fired again and another rolled to the side. A dog leaped up at the sound and Egan fired once more. The animal fell backward and rolled down the hill.

The dog on Rachel wouldn't let go of its prey, and was too close to her for Egan to shoot without a guarantee he wouldn't hit her. Running forward, he pulled the knife from the scabbard on his waist, then stabbed until the dog released her and lay motionless.

Rachel cowered there, covered in blood, the hairbrush clutched in her bloody hand. "It's okay," Egan told her. "I'm here."

"There's…more," she gasped.

He raised his head and saw Izzy McCray and two more dogs about twenty yards away. Egan's gun lay on the grass and he immediately reached for it.

"You killed my dogs, you bastard!" Izzy screamed.

"You're next!" Egan shouted back. He fired over Izzy's head and he and the dogs retreated into the woods.

Rachel shook from head to toe and her teeth were chattering. Egan pried the brush from her hand and threw it on the ground. Seeing the green sweater, he reached for it. With a sleeve, he wiped blood from her face and her throat. "Calm down," he cooed, as if to a child. "I'm not going to let anything else happen to you. Take a deep breath. Take another."

"E-gan," she cried, and tears rolled from her eyes.

He dabbed blood from the scratches on her face and neck. Luckily, they didn't look deep. "Come on, we have to get out of here. That crazy fool might be waiting in the woods."

Rachel shook violently. Egan grabbed the duster and wrapped it around her. Then he looped her purse over his shoulder and lifted her into his arms. The rifle lay on the ground and he bent for it. Walking into the woods to where he'd dropped the canteen, he squatted and reached for it, while resting the rifle against his leg. He screwed off the top with his thumb and forefinger and put the canteen to her lips.

"Drink."

She raised her hands and he saw how bloody and scratched they were. His gut tightened at what had been done to her. He should never have left her. Damn!

After she finished, he screwed the top back on and let the canteen rest on her chest. Holding her close, he got to his feet with the rifle in hand and then took off into the woods, trying to walk as fast as he could.

"Where are we going?" She laid her head against him, her blond hair matted with blood.

"My great-great-great-grandparents settled on Yaupon Creek and their cabin is still there. I try to keep it up. It has a bed and the bare necessities, but you can rest and I can clean your wounds. The only problem is it's taking us farther from the ranch, but I think you need medical attention more right now."

"Do you think he's following us?"

Egan wanted to tell her no, but he wasn't sure about crazy Izzy, and he wanted to be honest with her. On the other hand, he didn't want to scare her to death. She'd been through enough for one day.

"Don't worry. I have my rifle and we'll be at the cabin in no time."

Egan thought he was in good shape, but by the time he saw the one-room log cabin nestled on the bank of the creek his muscles were tight and aching. Tall oaks and scrappy yaupons surrounded the place. The view from the front porch was the same as it had been over a hundred years ago. The lazy creek flowed like a pale ribbon and was inhabited by fish, frogs, snakes and turtles. Animals came to drink at different times of the day. Enormous live oaks and cedars shaded it. The yaupons had been cut back for a better view of the valley below.

The steps creaked as he put his weight on them. He needed to fix that, but never seemed to find the time. Juggling Rachel and the rifle, he managed to open the door and carry her inside. "Doin' What She Likes" by Blake Shelton blared loudly.

He laid her on the mattress of a single bed in a corner across from a stone fireplace.

"Where's that music coming from?" She curled up on an old patchwork quilt of his grandmother's.

"A transistor radio I keep on to discourage little critters from coming in. It works pretty good. If they hear a human voice, they go elsewhere."

"How clever."

"Yeah." He turned off the radio. "Rest," he told her. "I'm going outside to get more water."

She sat up, her eyes wild. "Egan…"

"It's okay. I'll be right outside. The only way in is through this front door and I'll have my eye on it. Just try to relax."

It didn't take him long to get the old pump working at the well. It had been repaired so many times, but still provided water. He filled the bucket and carried it inside, keeping his rifle in hand and a close eye on the surrounding woods as he did so. An armadillo rooted about and birds chirped. Other than that, it was just a normal day in the woods.

But it was anything but normal.

Chapter Three

Rachel's skin burned and she wanted to scream. But she feared if she started, she would never be able to stop. She kept her eyes open, because if she closed them, she could feel the dogs on her—their smelly breath, coarse fur and claws so sharp they'd ripped through her skin.

A scream clogged her throat and she pulled the duster closer around her. The woodsy, masculine, sweaty scent enveloped her, but it wasn't abrasive. It was soothing because it reminded her of Egan.

She kept her eyes on the door and soon he walked in with a bucket of water, which he set on the floor. Blood covered his shirt, but he didn't seem to notice it.

"I have to clean those wounds and see how bad they are."

She pushed herself to a sitting position and brushed her fingers through her blood-caked, tangled hair. Egan's hand touched her face and neck and she stilled. No one had ever touched her that way—gentle, caring and respectful.

"The skin is broken in several places and your neck has two punctures, but they don't look deep. I'll clean them with the water and then I can see better." He pulled a handkerchief from his back pocket and dipped it in the bucket. Looking at her, he added, "It might be best if you remove your blouse. Some of the scratches on your neck go down."

Without a second thought, she lifted the blouse over her head and exposed her breasts in a lacy pink bra. He seemed completely unmoved by the sight. Gently, he wiped and squeezed water over each scratch and wound until the liquid in the bucket was bloody. The cloth was cool on her skin, but an inner fire was building in her. With each stroke, she wanted to catch his hand and hold it to her breasts, to feel his touch in a more personal way. It probably was due to the trauma she'd been through, because she'd never reacted this way to any man before.

"I'm going to push on the neck bites to get them to bleed so it will cleanse the wounds of saliva and bacteria."

"Okay." She winced as his fingers pressed into her skin.

"I'm worried about rabies, even though Izzy takes very good care of those dogs. Still, they're in the woods all the time and a few skunks have tested positive for rabies. There's whiskey in the cabinet. Do you think you could stand it if I pour it over the scratches and bites? It'll kill whatever bacteria is there and it's all that I have available here. It'll sting, but…"

Rachel reached out and removed Egan's hat. He drew back slightly, which was his only reaction. "I can't see your eyes with your hat on," she said.

He lifted a dark eyebrow. "Is it necessary to see my eyes?"

"Most definitely."

He went to a small cabinet and came back with a bottle of whiskey. Handing it to her, he said, "You might want to drink some first."

"Straight?"

"It'll numb your senses."

"All righty."

She lifted the bottle and took a swig, swallowed and coughed as it burned her throat. Her eyes watered, but she took another drink.

"I have to get more water and rinse out the handkerchief. Sip it slowly or your eyes are going to bulge out. Evidently, you're not used to hard liquor."

"A margarita or a glass of merlot is more my style."

"I could've guessed."

She made a face and took another swig, coughing until she thought it was going to come up again. Lying back, she watched glittery rainbows float across the old wood beams of the ceiling. A numbness invaded her mind. She reached out for Egan's hand. His strong fingers closed around hers and she knew everything was going to be okay. Egan would take care of her. That seemed odd, since she'd been fighting for years for her independence. But with Egan it was different.

"I like you, Egan Rebel."

"Ma'am…"

A bubble of laughter erupted from her throat, and she thought if she could hear him say that word in that tone for the rest of her life, she would be in heaven.

EGAN WENT OUTSIDE for more water and rinsed the handkerchief until it was as clean as it was going to get. Back in the cabin Rachel was falling in and out of consciousness. He placed his hand on her forehead to see if she had a fever, but her skin was cool. She was just getting drunk and he had a feeling she didn't do that often. If ever.

"Ready?" he asked, squatting by the bed.

She drew a deep breath. "Yes."

He took the bottle from her and soaked the handkerchief. He started with the scratches on her hands and arms, where she'd fought the dogs. The moment the whiskey touched the open wounds she bit down on her lip to keep from screaming. He admired that. She had guts.

Quickly, he continued, making sure each scratch was covered with alcohol. She flinched when he did the ones on her face.

"Is it bad?"

"It'll heal in no time and you'll still be beautiful."

"Ah, you think I'm beautiful?"

He soaked the bites on her neck and she bit her lip again, preventing her from talking, which he thought was good. She was the most beautiful woman he'd ever seen. God had heaven in mind when he'd created her. Natural blond hair, blue eyes and model-like features. Everything about her was perfection, including her curved, feminine body. Touching her skin was an exercise in restraint. Egan had never felt anything so soft, supple and tempting. One scratch arrowed down to a breast and his hand slowed as he reached its fullness. He wanted to cup it, to feel its weight in his palm. With superhuman strength, he pulled away and screwed the top on the bottle of whiskey.

Standing, he unbuttoned his shirt and took it off. Then he whipped his T-shirt over his head and handed it to her. "Your blouse is ruined, but you can wear this." He wanted to cover up those breasts any way he could.

She tugged it over her head and pull the duster around her. "I'm so sleepy."

"It's the whiskey."

Her eyelashes were light brown and lay softly against her skin as a liquor-induced sleep claimed her. He touched her forehead one more time to make sure she didn't have a fever. Once he was sure of that, he walked outside to the long porch on the front of the cabin.

He sat on the stoop and stared at the creek and the valley below. If she had a fever, they'd have to leave quickly to get her medical attention. They could probably reach the ranch by noon if they walked at a steady pace. He'd let her sleep for a bit and then they'd start out.

Egan's emotions were all over the place and he couldn't think straight when he was around her. He'd never had this problem before. She was making him forget that he'd ever known Judge Hollister. But the memory always returned. Egan would never be able to forgive the man for what he'd done, and that meant he couldn't have any kind of relationship with his daughter.

Relationship?

Where did that come from? He wasn't planning a relationship with Rachel Hollister. He just wanted to get her back to wherever she belonged. And that wasn't with him.

He ran his hands up his face and took a deep breath. It would be a long time before the memory of those dogs clawing at her would fade. He'd been so afraid they would kill her. And that was unacceptable and terrifying. He was glad he'd gotten there when he had. Izzy was going to pay for this one way or another. Egan would call the sheriff just as soon as they made it back to the ranch. Izzy had trained those dogs to kill, and that wasn't safe for anyone.

Glancing down, Egan saw that his knife was in its sheath. He didn't even remember putting it there. The handle was covered with blood. He pulled it out and saw that the blade was, too. He got up and made his way to the well. There wasn't anything to clean it with but water. He scrubbed the dried blood with leaves and that did the trick. Slipping it back into its sheath, he knew he might have to use it again.

"Egan!"

His name echoed through the valley with mind-splitting terror. He ran back to the cabin and Rachel flew into his arms.

"Egan." She threw herself against him and held on, her body trembling. "I…thought…you'd left me here."

He stroked her back. "You know I wouldn't do that. Calm down. You just had a bad dream."

"Every time I close my eyes…"

"Shh." He led her to the bed. "How do you feel?"

She drew in a deep breath. "Better now that you're here."

"We need to start walking soon." He checked the scratches and bites on her neck. "Everything looks good." Touching her forehead, he added, "And you don't have a fever."

"Can we stay here a little while longer? I don't want to go back out there just yet."

"The sooner we leave, the faster we'll make it to the ranch."

She looked down at the scrapes on her hands. "I can't go home like this."

"Rachel, you've been through something horrific and you need your family."

She raised her eyes to his and they filled with tears. At the sight, his resolve weakened.

"I need you. I know that sounds crazy, but—" she shook her head "—it's the way I feel. Please, let's stay here just a little while longer and then I can face my family."

The pain in her voice got to him, but he had to be honest. "Rachel, you hardly know me. You're clinging to me because you're afraid."

"I know," she said in a dejected voice. She got up and walked to the doorway. "Oh, look at that view. I can understand why your ancestors chose this spot." She walked out onto the porch and he followed. Six deer were at the creek, drinking. Quietly, she eased onto the stoop as if mesmerized by the sight.

"I'd love to paint that," she whispered.

He sat beside her. "Obviously, you're an artist, because you seem to want to paint everything."

"Yes. I teach art in a private girls' school in New York."

At that moment, he realized Rachel was way, way out of his league. Yet it was hard to explain the feelings that had ignited between them. They had nothing in common and she was... He didn't even want to think the words, so he stared off to the creek below.

They sat in silence for a long time, both comfortable with each other, but he was very aware of her breasts pressing against his T-shirt.

Finally, she turned to him. "I'm so hungry."

"I think I left some canned stuff here. I'll check." He went inside and left her to her musings. He found a can of SpaghettiOs and one of ravioli. After opening them, he carried them outside with two plastic spoons.

"We try not to leave anything up here because it attracts foraging animals. Canned stuff is the only thing they won't drag off." They sat on the stoop and ate like two kids with a treat.

"This is delicious," she said. "Or I'm just really hungry."

"You're really hungry." He spooned ravioli into his mouth and it wasn't bad. "When we were kids, my mom used to buy this by the case. On the ranch, you're always busy and kids are always hungry. It was a go-to staple."

"How many brothers do you have?"

"Six. My mom had seven kids in eight years. Jude and Phoenix were born in the same year."

"I can't even imagine that." Rachel licked the spoon.

"Jude and Phoenix were in my class. Jude dated Paige forever. Did they ever get married?"

"No," Egan said shortly. He didn't want to discuss his family.

"That's sad. They were so in love."

"Mmm." Paige had chosen a career over love and family. Egan didn't understand that, but he felt for his brother.

"There was another brother a year ahead of me and he was a bull rider."

"That's Paxton."

"The girls were crazy about him."

Egan ate the last of the ravioli. "Yeah, Paxton's a ladies' man."

Rachel glanced sideways at him. "Are you?"

"Not close. My mother calls me the loner in the family. I'd rather be out here in these woods than in a crowded room of people."

She pointed the spoon at him. "You see, I would have guessed that about you. You're a quiet thinker and Paxton has nothing on you in looks, except his hair is lighter. But personally, I prefer dark hair and serious thinking men."

The conversation was getting way out of his comfort zone. Egan took the can and spoon from her.

"What are you going to do with those?"

"Bury them so animals won't be tempted into the cabin."

"Doesn't the music keep them out?"

"Not if they smell food."

A shovel lay on the edge of the porch. He reached for it and walked into the woods. She didn't panic that he was leaving her, but he could feel her eyes on him. He took his time because he had to gather his thoughts. They were getting too close, sharing too much.

After a few minutes he returned to the cabin, determined to keep things on an impersonal level.

"It's so peaceful and quiet here. I love it."

"But it's far away from what you're used to."

"Yeah." She rubbed her thumb over the dried blood on her jeans.

"Rachel, we need to talk."

She glanced at him, but didn't say anything.

"You didn't do anything wrong. You didn't cause your mother's death, so there's no reason to fear going home."

"Then why do I feel this way?"

"You'll feel differently when you talk to your family. They're who you need right now. Not me. I'm a stranger."

Her eyes held his and he felt as if he was swimming in the blue waters of South Padre Island, warm, inviting and irresistible.

"You don't feel like a stranger to me. I trusted you from the moment I looked into your eyes."

"You know nothing about me."

"But I do. You saved my life, and I don't think there's anything you can say about yourself that will change my mind."

There was only one way to change her mind and he had to do it. "I spent time in prison. I'm an ex-con."

She wiped her mouth with the back of her hand. "Do I have sauce on my face?"

Exasperation replaced his patience. "Yes."

With her tongue she licked around her lips. He watched the action as if she had hypnotized him. Desire uncurled in his stomach.

"Could I have some water, please?"

He grunted and went to refill the bucket before he said something he would regret. But this wasn't over. She had to face facts. They had to start walking soon.

When he returned to the stoop, she wasn't there. He found her inside sitting on the bed. He handed her the ladle from the bucket and she drank. He was trying his best not to stare at her in his T-shirt. Even after being attacked by dogs, she looked better in it than he ever had.

He set the bucket on the floor. "Rachel…"

"I'm tired, Egan, and I just want to rest."

"You can't spend the rest of your life avoiding your family."

"Don't lecture me." Anger coated her words for the first time. He was getting a reaction. That was good. He had to keep pushing.

"I'm not your hero. I'm just a man who got caught up in your life, and the sooner I get you back to your family, the sooner I can get back to mine. And please don't weave a fantasy around me. I'm not a fairy-tale type guy."

"I know," she snapped. "You told me. You're an ex-con. Do you expect me to run away screeching in terror?"

"No, but I expect you to understand that we need to go now."

She stretched out on the bed. "But I'm so tired and I feel weak. Please let me rest. Then we'll do what you want."

Her voice was low and troubling. He reached out to touch her forehead. "You don't have a fever."

She pulled the duster around her. "I just need to rest. My nerves are all tied in knots."

Egan gave up. He couldn't push her if she didn't feel well. Glancing outside, he saw the shadows lengthening. It was getting late. Too late for them to start walking. They'd have to spend the night here.

There was an old wooden rocker in the cabin and he pulled it forward and sat in it. "Do you feel sick to your stomach?"

"No."

"Do you have a headache?"

"No, but you're giving me one."

He let that pass. "In a little while I'll need to put whiskey on the scratches and bites again."

"Okay."

She closed her eyes and he thought she was asleep. But then her voice came, soft and inquisitive, "What did you do that you had to go to prison? You're so gentle I just can't imagine you doing anything bad."

"It was a long time ago and I don't like to talk about it."

Using her hands as a pillow beneath the side of her face, she got comfy and asked, "How old were you?"

"I was twenty and in college." He hadn't meant to answer, but the words slipped out.

"In college, kids drink a lot. Did you do something while you were drunk?"

He hated the memories as bad as anything in his life, but something in him had a need to tell her so she would understand.

"Yes." That was the only word that came out of his dry mouth, and he hoped she would drop the subject.

"I told you my deep dark secret, so you can talk to me. What we say here stays here."

"We're not in Vegas."

Her lips curved into an enchanting smile. "That would be nice to share with you."

"Rachel, please stop seeing me as someone you'd like to have a relationship with."

"Why?"

He had to tell her. It was the only way to stop the fantasy in her head. "I was twenty years old and enjoying college life, like all kids that age. It was the end of the school year and summer beckoned. Celebration parties were going on everywhere. I attended one with my friend and got drunk, way too drunk. He hooked up with someone and I didn't have a ride home, so these two guys said they would drop me off at my dorm. The next thing I knew I was in a hospital bed under arrest."

She sat up, her eyes enormous. "What happened?"

"Seemed the two idiots decided to rob a liquor store. They were high on crack and killed the man inside. I was passed out drunk in the backseat. I didn't really know these guys and had no idea of their plans."

"But you didn't do anything."

"No, I didn't. Even after the toxicology report came back and showed I didn't have any crack in my system, only booze, the judge didn't buy it. My friends at the party testified that I had just gotten a ride home from them. The judge thought I needed to be taught a lesson about how to choose my friends and how to have more control over what I drink. And to be more responsible. He could have given me probation and community service, but he sentenced me to a year in prison."

"How awful. Oh, Egan, I'm so sorry you had to go through that." Before he could stop her she slipped off the bed and onto his lap. He tensed. She'd blindsided him with her reaction and he didn't want to react. He wanted her to…

Her arms went around his neck and she rested her forehead against the side of his. "That must have been terrible for a young man."

He closed his eyes, breathing in the scent of her and the fragrance that lingered in her hair. All feminine. All intoxicating. All he wanted at that moment.

Then from the deepest, darkest part of his soul the

words came, words he'd never said to anyone, not his brothers, not his mother, not anyone.

"It was hell on earth. When they drove us into the prison and those big gates closed behind the van, I knew I was in the worst possible place. Everything was taken from me. I was stripped of my clothes, my pride, my life. Then they ushered me down long halls with cell after cinder-block cell. I was pushed into one, and as the steel door clanged shut, I was frightened beyond anything I've ever felt in my life. There was no way out. I was trapped like an animal, with other animals who had no qualms about inflicting pain. They called me pretty boy. I made a friend, Jericho, and he saved me many times. But daily I lived in fear for my life. I can't tell you how that changes a man. I—"

"Shh." She kissed his cheek. "Don't relive it. You don't have to. You're free now." Her mouth trailed to the corner of his and he turned his head to meet her lips. He groaned at the sweetness of her and deepened the kiss. His arms tightened around her and the earth stood still as, for the first time, he let someone else share the pain of that time. Allowed someone to console him. She tasted of spaghetti and liquor, and it was the best taste he'd ever had. He wanted more and more and more...

His hand trailed beneath the T-shirt to caress the softness of her breast. Somewhere in the rational part of his mind, he knew this was wrong. He had to stop it. Now!

"Rach..."

"How long did you have to stay there?"

He withdrew his hand from her breast. He had to gain control. "My mother hired another attorney and he collected more evidence, damning evidence. The crime had happened in Waco, Texas, and the judge was a visiting one. My lawyer at the time had advised me to let the judge decide my sentence instead of going through a jury trial. My family and I agreed. Being familiar with my family and Horseshoe, the judge should have recused himself. He chose not to. My new lawyer brought this out in an appeal and the original sentence was overturned. I was finally exonerated, the charges were dropped and I was released after three months. But three months scarred me for life."

"Egan…"

"I'm telling you this so you'll understand where I'm coming from when I say you and I will never have any kind of relationship. I will get you back to your family, but that's it."

She went still in his arms. "I don't understand. I don't think any less of you for what happened, and you shouldn't, either."

"We've known each other for about twenty-four hours now. We should never have met, but sometimes fate is cruel."

"I know you're going somewhere with this, but for the life of me I have no idea what it is."

Egan removed his arm from around her waist and studied the blood under his fingernails. "The judge who sent me to prison to make a point, to teach me a lesson, was Hardison Hollister, your father."

Chapter Four

Rachel slipped from his lap, shaking her head. "No, that's not true. My father was known for his honest and fair decisions. He wouldn't do something like that."

Egan stood—tall, rigid and defiant. "He was also known for his stiff and unrelenting decisions dictated by his high moral code. The only thing I was guilty of was underage drinking. But he said I'd made choices and I had to be accountable for them. And since my family had a history of violence, he couldn't just let it go. I needed to learn a lesson, and the only way to do that was to think about my actions in prison. There was nothing fair about his words or his judgment." Egan swung away and strolled outside in the dwindling light, as if saying the words took every ounce of energy he had.

Rachel sat on the bed, speechless. Her father had been a judge for many years and she'd never thought much about his occupation. But his decisions affected lives… like Egan's. Growing up, she'd seen little of her father. He was always busy, in court or out of town at political events, or sitting in as a visiting judge. Her mother had always been the mainstay in Rachel's life. She drew a deep breath and curled up on the bed.

Coming home was turning into a nightmare. How much guilt could she load onto her poor old soul? Egan's pain was something she could feel, but he didn't want her sympathy or her comforting words. What could she say to him?

Even after everything he'd told her, those feelings she had for him hadn't changed. A lot more questions about her father lingered, though.

From the bed, she could see Egan sitting on the stoop, staring into the darkness and battling the demons inside him. The moonlight shone a path between them. As if he sensed her stare, he got up and walked back into the house.

"I have to put alcohol on your wounds," he said, his voice a rough edge of reality. No matter how much he wanted to ignore her, he couldn't. Her safety and welfare were important to him and that said more about him than any sentence he could have been given.

He went to the cabinet and pulled out something. A split second later there was light in the cabin.

"Oh." She was startled by the brightness.

"It's a kerosene lantern," he said. "It belonged to my grandparents and I use it for light sometimes." He placed it on the floor, grabbed the whiskey bottle, sat beside her and began to dab at the scratches on her arms and neck.

"Where did you get that piece of cloth?"

"I cut it off of your top."

"I didn't see you do that."

"Just sit quietly." He soaked the scratches on her hands, arms and neck. It didn't sting as badly this time. With the flickering lamp and the darkness crowding in, the setting and the moment could have been romantic. But there was nothing romantic about their situation.

His hand lingered on her neck and moved gently to her cheek. His touch was soft, almost a caress. She imagined he made love the same way—gently, with total concentration and attention to detail. Without thinking, she leaned her face into his hand.

He cleared his throat. "You'll have to remove the T-shirt so I can soak the scratches on your chest."

The shirt came off with one easy movement. He dabbed at the scratches, his hand lingering over the fullness of her breast.

A ragged breath caught in her throat. "Touch me."

"I am touching you." His voice came out hoarse.

"No." She reached up and removed his hat. "I mean like you want to touch me."

He stood abruptly. "That's done. Now get some rest."

Pretending she hadn't spoken wasn't going to stop her. "Egan..."

"Don't say anything else. We've said enough."

"There's a chemistry between us that has nothing to do with my father. It has to do with us."

He sighed. "Rachel, there's nothing between us. We're two strangers who met by accident. That's it."

"You wanted to touch my breast in a more intimate way. Don't deny it, because I felt it."

He turned from putting the whiskey bottle in the cabinet. "You're a beautiful woman. What man wouldn't be attracted to you? I'm human. That's all."

There wasn't much she could say after that. She had to stop fighting for something that was never going to be. She'd met him only yesterday. Once she was away from him, her world would right itself and she would forget about him. But something inside her told her differently. Forgetting Egan wouldn't be easy.

"Go to sleep." He blew out the lantern and moved toward the door.

"Aren't you going to sleep, too?"

"Maybe later. I don't sleep much. I'll sit on the stoop for a while."

"Do you think that man is still out there?"

"Izzy is somewhere, but I doubt if he's hiding in these woods. We'll be long gone before he sets out to track us in the morning. Don't worry. Just rest."

She tugged the T-shirt over her head and curled up on the bed, her eyes on his rigid back. As she moved, her hand touched something. His hat. He'd forgotten his hat. That had to be a first, and she wondered if he slept in it when he was home. She doubted it. In that moment, she knew she wanted to know a lot more about Egan Rebel.

EGAN KEPT THE RIFLE by his side. He wasn't as sure about old Izzy as he'd pretended to be to Rachel. The man was crazy and could pop up at any moment, but Egan was ready for him.

An owl hooted through the chirp of crickets and the night wore on. It had to be close to midnight. He didn't wear a watch anymore, since he'd got it caught on a string of a bale of hay and almost had his arm ripped off. His phone was now his watch, but it was in his duster and he wasn't going to disturb Rachel. Besides, there was no signal.

He flexed his fingers, recalling the smoothness of her skin against his fingertips. She was right. He wanted to touch her in a more intimate way, and that feeling angered him. There were so many girls in the world and the one that he could never have was the one he was drawn to. There was no way on God's green earth he could see himself dating Rachel Hollister. But she was tempting. He'd just leave it at that.

A long walk was ahead of him in the morning, so he had to get some rest. The rocker was preferable to sitting on the stoop. He tiptoed inside and lightly closed the door. The rocker was as hard as the stoop, but he'd adjust.

"Sleep on the bed, Egan. You need to rest." Her voice was soft, yet strong.

Being male and in control, he stretched out on the bed and his body relaxed.

"Do you want your hat?" she asked. "It's right here."

A grin spread across his face, but he was the only one who knew that. "No. I actually don't sleep in my hat or my boots at home."

"I didn't think so." She moved around on the mattress, bumping into him.

"What are you doing?"

"Taking off my sneakers. I can't sleep in them another night."

After a moment, she curled up next to him and it was a little too close for his comfort. But he was in control, he told himself again.

"Did you take your boots off?"

"No." He wanted to be ready in case Izzy made an appearance. Egan wouldn't tell her that, though.

Finally, the silence was wonderful as they gave in to the tiredness of their bodies.

"I'm really sorry for what you went through, Egan."

"I know. Just go to sleep, and tomorrow you'll be back with your family."

"I'm excited and dreading it at the same time."

"Just relax and everything will go smoothly."

There was a long pause. "Can I see you before I go back to New York?"

He moved restlessly, not wanting to have this conversation. "I'd rather not."

"I never felt about anyone the way I feel about you.

I know you don't want to hear that, but I'm just being honest."

"Rachel…"

"I'm very aware you don't want to be attracted to me."

"You got it."

"You don't have to be cruel."

"I'm not. I'm just being honest, as you said." He flipped onto his side and waited for her to stop talking. They didn't have anything else to talk about, and the less they said, the better it was for both of them.

"You're very stubborn."

"Mmm."

Egan must've fallen asleep, because the next thing he knew, his back was warm and he was uncomfortable. A raspy sound came from Rachel. He leaned over and touched her forehead. Damn! Her skin was red-hot. She had a fever. He jumped from the bed and gently shook her.

"Rachel, wake up. We have to go."

"Is it morning?" she asked sleepily. "My head hurts and I feel funny."

"I must've missed one of the scratches because you're burning up with fever. You need medical attention, so we have to leave now. Can you put on your sneakers?"

"What?"

"Put on your shoes. I'm going outside for water." He grabbed his hat and slammed it onto his head.

When he came back, Rachel was slumped over on the bed, asleep. He shook her awake. "Come on. You have to wake up." He held the canteen to her lips. "Drink this."

"Oh, it tastes wonderful."

He ripped her ruined top into strips and soaked them in water. As he secured the wet cloth around her neck, she drew back. "What's that?"

"Something cool to bring down your fever."

"It feels good."

He searched for her sneakers on the floor. The lantern was a few feet away, but he didn't have time to light it. They had to go. He'd never put shoes on a woman before and found it a chore. "Help me here, and stop scrunching up your toes."

"I can put them on myself," she complained.

But he had them on her in seconds and laced them up. He helped her to her feet. "We have to start walking."

"Didn't you say we couldn't walk in the dark?"

"We don't have any option now. You need a doctor."

He fished his phone out of the duster and shoved it into a pocket of his jeans. Grabbing his rifle, he ushered her to the door. He didn't take anything else; it would only slow them down. Once they were outside, he closed the door. They never locked it. There wasn't a lock, even if he'd wanted to. This far back in the woods, if anyone wanted to break in they'd find a way. Besides, there was nothing valuable in the cabin but memories.

He filled the canteen one more time and looped the strap over his neck and shoulder. "Stay right behind me," he told her as they started off.

She didn't answer.

"Rachel?"

"I'm so hot."

"I know. That's why we're walking."

It had to be about 5:00 a.m. and it was slow going. He'd cut a trail to the cabin a long time ago, but there were still some low-hanging branches and overgrown yaupons. Rachel stayed close behind him and he made sure none of the branches hit her.

The morning was cool. Soon birds began to chirp, so daylight wasn't far away. Suddenly, Rachel fell into him, and Egan turned quickly to catch her before she injured herself further.

"Uh-oh."

"It's okay," he said, holding her up.

"I'm dizzy and feel sick to my stomach," she mumbled.

He lifted her into his arms and began to walk at a faster pace. He had to get help soon. As they reached the ridge, the morning sun peeped over the treetops like a golden angel flapping her wings. He began to run. Since he could see clearly, he wasn't afraid of falling. But after a mile or so he dropped to his knees, needing to rest.

Placing Rachel on the green grass, he took a couple deep breaths and then reached for the canteen. He soaked the cloth and her body with it.

"My leg hurts."

Her right leg was swollen at the calf. Damn! With his knife, he slit her jeans to ease the pressure. He immediately saw the infected red scratch. He'd missed it. He said another cuss word under his breath.

"I'm floating, Egan. Don't let me float away."

He stroked her sweat-soaked hair away from her face. "I won't. Just hold on, sweet lady. We're getting close." Leaning back, he pulled out his phone and checked for a signal. There still wasn't one.

"I like that."

"What?"

"Sweet lady."

He hadn't even realized he'd called her that. It had just slipped out.

"I like ma'am, too," she mumbled. "Some women don't like it. They feel it insults them, but they've never heard you say it."

She was delirious. A long sigh escaped Egan and he got to his feet with Rachel in his arms. The rifle he had to leave behind, because he could no longer carry it. He kept the phone in his hand. Soon he should get a signal. He had to.

HARDY HOLLISTER TIPTOED down the stairs, careful not to make a sound. The baby and Angie were finally asleep. In the kitchen, he made coffee. His cell buzzed and he started to ignore it, but he was the DA, so he pulled it from his robe. It was his friend Wyatt, the sheriff.

He clicked on. "This had better be good, Wyatt. We've been up most of the night with Trey."

"I remember those days. I'm so glad J.W. sleeps through the night now. It'll get better."

"What's up this early in the morning?"

"Is Rachel coming home for a visit?"

"Not that I'm aware of. I talked to her a few days ago and she didn't say anything about coming home. Why?"

"I got a call from the highway patrol. A rental car was found at the back of Rebel Ranch, a deeply wooded area with not a house around for miles. The car was rented in Austin to Rachel Hollister on Friday. A suitcase with clothes was in the backseat. Her name is on the tags."

"What? That doesn't make any sense."

Judge Hollister walked into the kitchen, obviously looking for a cup of coffee. "Just a minute," Hardy said to Wyatt. "Dad, have you talked to Rachel?"

The judge pulled out a chair and sat at the table, sipping the hot brew. "No. She's mad at me because I chewed her out about not coming home. She probably won't talk to me for a couple weeks."

Hardy picked up his cell again. "Dad hasn't heard from her, either. This doesn't sound right and it's not like Rachel to do something like that."

"I hate to give you any more bad news, but there's a witness who said he saw a man drag a woman from the car into the woods."

Hardy's hand tightened on the phone. "Can he identify the woman?"

"No, but he identified the man."

"Who."

"Egan Rebel."

"Something's not right, Wyatt. Egan's a model citizen and I don't think he knows Rachel."

"Rachel?" The judge shot to his feet. "What about Rachel?"

"I'm coming in, Wyatt. I just have to get dressed." Hardy laid his phone down and faced his dad. He told him exactly what Wyatt had said. It wasn't a time to keep secrets. His father was a strong man.

"Egan Rebel. I sent him to prison years ago. He said he'd get even, and this could be his way of getting back at me. He better not hurt my daughter or he'll never see the light of day again."

"Calm down, Dad." Hardy picked up his phone again. "I'll call her apartment in New York. This has to be a big mistake. She would want us to know if she was coming home."

It didn't take long for Rachel's roommate, Della, to answer the phone. From her sleepy voice, he knew he'd awakened her.

"I'm sorry to call so early. This is Hardy Hollister, Rachel's brother. I'm trying to get in touch with her."

"What? Rachel left on Friday to visit her family in Horseshoe."

"Are you sure? She didn't call to let us know."

"She wanted it to be a surprise."

"Thank you, Della. She never arrived and we're worried. I'll call you back as soon as I find out anything."

"Please do."

THE WIND PICKED UP and seemed to be pushing Egan backward, but he kept going. He punched the phone repeatedly, praying for it to light up. When it finally did, he almost tripped and fell. He sank to the ground, still holding Rachel, who was now completely limp.

"Egan...Egan...are you there?" It was Rico.

His body sagged as he answered. "Can you hear me?"

"Yeah. Man, where have you been? The whole family's looking for you."

"I'm west of the big coastal hay patch, in direct line to the barn where Jude makes his saddles. I have a casualty. She's been attacked by dogs and needs to get to a hospital. Call 911 and bring a Polaris Ranger out here. I'll keep walking until you get here. Do you hear me?"

"Got it." The good thing about Rico was he never asked questions. Egan struggled to his feet and started walking again. Help was on the way. He relaxed just a little.

"Egan..." Rachel murmured. "Don't let me float away."

He held her a bit tighter, picked up his pace and then slowed when he saw the ranger speeding toward him. Sinking to his knees, Egan clutched Rachel in his arms.

"Help is on the way, sweet lady. We made it. Can you hear me?"

"E-gan..." Her flushed face rested against his chest, her lips barely moving.

His brothers Falcon and Quincy jumped from the ranger. Falcon was the oldest and had taken control of the ranch after their father's death. He wasn't quite the same after his wife had left him and their three-month-old daughter. He was strict and stern and gave no one any leeway, not even his little girl.

Quincy was the second son, with dark hair and eyes similar to Egan. He was the peacemaker in the family. He'd taken it upon his broad shoulders to keep unity among the brothers, which was not an easy task, since they seemed to have wildness branded onto their souls.

"Is an ambulance on the way?" Egan asked.

Falcon and Quincy squatted beside him, staring at Rachel. "What happened?" Falcon asked.

"Is an ambulance on the way?" Egan repeated.

"Rico's waiting at the ranch entrance, but I talked to the dispatch lady and told her it might be best to send a medical helicopter, since you were so far out on the range." His brow knotted. "She looks as if she's been in a fight or something. What are those scratches from?"

"Help me get her in the ranger," Egan said. "I'll explain later."

He stood once again with Rachel in his arms, but paused when he heard the sound of a chopper.

Quincy waved his arms, guiding the helicopter in. Things happened quickly after it landed in a whirlwind of dust. Two paramedics jumped out with a stretcher and Egan laid Rachel on it. They immediately began to assess her condition.

"What happened?" one of them asked.

"She was attacked by dogs. A scrape on her right calf is infected."

The other paramedic talked on the phone and then glanced at Egan. "Do you know who owns the dogs?"

"Isadore McCray of Horseshoe."

"Rabies is a concern, but we have to get her to the hospital now. Her temperature is 103."

As they rolled the stretcher to the chopper, Rachel stirred. "Egan..."

He went to her. "Everything's going to be okay. They're taking you to the hospital and your family will meet you there." Egan glanced at the paramedic. "Her name is Rachel Hollister and her father is Judge Hardison Hollister of Horseshoe. He shouldn't be too difficult to locate."

"E-gan..."

"Shh. You're going to be fine." He brushed wet hair from her forehead.

"Don't let me float away."

Egan's throat closed up and he stood there in silence as they loaded her onto the chopper. The blades began to swirl, the force of the draft almost knocking him off his feet. His hat blew away and he let it go. He kept staring at the chopper as it lifted up and disappeared into the blue sky.

Just as quickly as she'd arrived in his life, Rachel was gone. He should feel relief, but what he was feeling he couldn't describe. It had to be the tiredness that was pulling him down. When he could no longer see the helicopter, he whispered, "Goodbye, sweet lady."

Chapter Five

Wyatt frowned as Hardy walked into his office.

"Did you locate Rachel?"

The sheriff stood, anger in every line of his tall body. "I've had other things to keep me occupied." He picked up a piece of paper and slapped it onto the desk. "I have a warrant signed by Judge Henley for Egan Rebel's arrest."

"What? How did that happen so fast?"

"Your father made a phone call. Judge Henley was in church, but he left and went to his office and drew up the warrant himself and delivered it to me. I don't like being a puppet for your father, Hardy. I don't run my office that way."

"Wyatt, I'm sorry. I had no idea he would make a phone call. I told him I would handle it, but as always, he never listens to me."

Wyatt picked up the warrant. "I either arrest Egan or disobey a judge's direct order. I could lose my badge over this."

"Dad is worried about Rachel, and I am, too."

"That's no reason to arrest an innocent man."

"You said you had a witness who saw Egan drag Rachel from the car."

"Isadore McCray is not a reliable witness. The Rebels and the McCrays have been feuding for years, and I need to investigate this before any warrant is issued." Wyatt picked up another paper. "Also, I have a warrant to search the premises. How do you think that's going to go, Hardy, with Kate Rebel and her gun-toting sons? This is not my kind of justice and I resent your father's involvement."

"My sister could be in danger and that's all I can think about right now."

Wyatt reached for his hat and jammed it on his head. "I'm going out to the Rebel Ranch. I'll let you know what happens."

"I'll go with you," Hardy volunteered.

"No. I've had all the Hollister involvement I need."

Stuart, a deputy, stood. "I'll go with you, Sheriff."

"I'm going alone." Wyatt headed for the door. He glanced back at Hardy. "Tell your father to stay out of my business."

EGAN HAD A long shower, washed his hair, shaved and changed clothes. He was exhausted and thought of taking a nap, but wanted to call the hospital to check on Rachel. By now, her family should have been notified.

Falcon and Quincy, followed by Jude and Elias, burst through the front door. Paxton and Phoenix trailed behind. Egan had no idea what was going on, for all his brothers to suddenly arrive at his house.

There were four houses on the Rebel property. Their mother, Falcon and his daughter, Jude, and his son lived in the big log house at the front of the ranch. The house his parents had first lived in stood about a hundred yards behind it. Quincy, Elias and Egan lived there. Their grandfather's home was about fifty yards away, and they took turns staying with him because Grandpa Abe's memory was slipping. No one told him that, though. And Cupcake, as they called Falcon's daughter, also helped with her great-grandpa. She had a way with him. Paxton and Phoenix, Egan's rodeo brothers, occupied the bunkhouse, which they had redone. Jericho lived in the bunkhouse, also.

"Get your things. You have to go," Falcon shouted.

"Wh-what?"

Elias went into Egan's room and came out with a carryall. "You don't have much time, brother. Hurry."

"Just hold it a minute. What's going on?"

"The sheriff is at the main house and has a warrant for your arrest," Quincy told him. "Mom said for you to hide out in the old cellar. We'll get you out of Horseshoe just as soon as we can."

For a bizarre moment, Egan thought he had taken that nap and was dreaming. This would be a nightmare, though—like many he'd experienced in recent years.

"I'm not going anywhere until someone tells me what's going on."

"The sheriff says he has a witness who saw you drag Rachel Hollister from her car. You're being charged with kidnapping, and he wants to know Rachel's whereabouts." Falcon filled Egan in on the even more bizarre details. He was being charged with something he hadn't done. Again! A feeling of déjà vu came over him and fear gnawed at his insides. But he wouldn't give in to it.

"This is crazy. Did you tell him Rachel is in a hospital in Temple?"

"Mom's not telling him anything. She just wants the sheriff off our property and you in hiding."

Egan stiffened. "I'm not running. I didn't do anything. They can check it out at the hospital. Who's claiming I dragged Rachel from the car?"

"The sheriff wouldn't say. He's demanding to talk to you."

Egan turned toward the door. "Well, then, that's what he's going to get."

Paxton and Phoenix stood in front of the door. Paxton was broad shouldered and muscled. He was a bull rider and tough, as was Phoenix, though Phoenix was smaller in size. It'd been a long time since Egan had fought Paxton, but anger was building inside him like steam from a kettle and any minute he was going to blow and take anyone with him who was standing in front of him. Fate was too cruel for words. Today he wasn't in the mood to let the fickle cousin of the devil ruin his life for a second time.

"You're not leaving, Egan," Paxton said, straightening his shoulders for a fight. "Mom's orders."

Egan stared into dark eyes much like his own. "I'm not running like a coward, Pax. You got that? You either move or I'm going right through you."

"We don't need to fight among ourselves." Quincy moved to stand between them. "Mom's upset about this, Egan. She doesn't want to see you go to jail again."

"I don't, either, but I'm not hiding out like a criminal. Mom has to understand that."

Quincy lifted his shoulders and nodded to Paxton. His brother stepped away from the door, as did Phoenix.

Paxton pointed a finger at Quincy. "This is on you when Mom rains holy hell down on us."

Egan walked out the door and down the steps, leaving his brothers arguing. But he didn't take many steps before he knew they were right behind him. Jericho wasn't in sight and Egan wondered about that. His friend was very protective and Egan figured he'd be leading the charge to hide him.

At the back door to the big house, he stopped short. Jericho stood there with a shotgun in his hand. Egan had just gone through this with his brothers and he was growing tired of fighting a losing battle.

"Step aside, Jericho. This is my business and I can handle it. I'm not that scared kid I was fourteen years ago."

"I've got your back, man."

"I know and I appreciate that. But right now I need you to back me up when I say I haven't done anything. I need you to stand beside me and support me. And that means I'm not running. I'm not hiding. I'm facing whatever hell is waiting for me."

Jericho nodded and Egan went through the back door. His parents had built the log house about twenty years ago. It had six bedrooms, five baths and plenty of room for seven brothers to grow up in.

The large kitchen was decorated in candy-apple red, with black granite counters and pine cabinets. The table sat ten and had long benches on each side. Everyone had a place. His father had crafted the table himself because he'd wanted one big enough to seat his whole family. Dinner together was a must for his parents.

Voices could be heard from the den. Egan stopped for a moment to listen, figured it was best to know what he was walking into.

"You're not taking my son, Sheriff. You're on private property and I want you to leave."

"Miss Kate, I've known you all my life and I promise you I will be fair with Egan. I just want to talk to him and investigate what has happened to Rachel Hollister. According to a witness, he was the last person to see her."

"Let me make myself clear. You're not taking my son off this ranch. I will die before I let you railroad him once again."

"Miss Kate—"

"Your promises mean nothing to me. Judge Hollister has too much power in this town."

"I understand your concern, but—"

"You heard the lady, Sheriff. It's time for you to go." That was Grandpa Abe, who'd taught John Rebel and his sons how to ride, rope and be cowboys. There wasn't anything Egan's grandpa didn't know about ranching, and he'd spent all his life here on Rebel Ranch. He'd turned over the reins of the ranch to his son many years ago. These days Grandpa was sailing close to senility. He was still a tough old bird and never bent to any man. A few women, but never a man.

The sounds of guns cocking echoed from the timbers of the house. Egan peeped around the corner and saw his brothers and Jericho standing near the French patio doors with guns in their hands. Damn! He had to stop this.

"Tell your boys to put their guns down."

"My sons are in their home and have a right to do as they wish."

"You're making this hard, Miss Kate. Hiding Egan is not going to help him. I need to find out what happened to Rachel Hollister. That's all I'm asking, for just a few words with Egan."

"Then why bring a warrant?"

The sheriff paused and his mother picked up on it. "Like I said, Judge Hollister has too much power and I can't trust anything you say."

"You can, Miss Kate. If Egan is innocent, I will bring him home safe and sound. If not, he has to face the consequences. My gut instinct is saying something odd is going on here. But I have to talk to Egan to sort everything out."

The clanging of the steel doors, the roar of raucous laughter and vile cuss words echoed through Egan's head.

He couldn't go back to prison. This time it would kill him. He'd told Jericho he was stronger, and now he had to prove it, because he had nothing to hide. He was innocent. The last time he'd been, too. But he couldn't let that thought drag him down. He stepped away from the door frame and walked into the room like the strong man he was today.

"No, Egan," his mother shouted, motioning for him to go back. His brothers stepped forward, preventing the sheriff from reaching him.

Egan pushed through a wall of solid muscle and hard bones to face the sheriff. He appreciated his brothers' willingness to fight for him, but he had to do this alone. As he stood there, he could feel their breath on his neck.

Staring at Wyatt, he said, "Rachel Hollister is in a hospital in Temple. She was taken there by a medical helicopter early this morning."

"What happened to her?"

Egan told the story as he knew it. He didn't lie or embellish.

Wyatt placed his hands on his hips. "She was attacked by Isadore McCray's dogs?"

"Yes. I had to shoot four to keep them from killing her."

Wyatt reached for his phone on his belt. "I have to call the hospital to verify this."

"Go ahead."

Egan glanced at his mother and could see she was unhappy. Kate Rebel was about five feet two inches tall, with graying brown hair. All her sons feared and respected her. She'd grown strong from adversity and she had continued the ranch legacy their father had started. They all knew their mother ruled.

At times, her voice was gentle and soft, encouraging

and supporting them. Other times, it could stop them in their tracks and make sweat pop out on their foreheads. Above all that, Kate Rebel protected her sons with a vengeance.

Wyatt shoved his phone back into its case on his belt. "Your story checks out. Rachel is in the hospital, but she's sedated and can't tell her side of the story." He looked at Egan. "Until I can talk to her I'm asking you to come with me peacefully, no handcuffs. I have a warrant and I can't ignore that, but I promise you justice this time."

"How much is your justice worth, Sheriff Carson?" his mother asked. "A phone call from Judge Hollister?"

"If Rachel verifies Egan's story, I will release him immediately."

"You see, Sheriff, I'm not that trusting. My son is not leaving this ranch."

"You heard her," Grandpa said.

"Mr. Rebel, I have an eyewitness and a warrant and—"

"Funny thing about eyewitnesses." Grandpa pulled off his worn cowboy hat and scratched his head. "Back in 1989, an eyewitness said I was shacked up with Clive Gundry's wife down at the We-No-Tell-Motel. Ms. Gundry was a fine-looking woman and any man would be as happy as a pig in slop to shack up with her, but you see, it wasn't me. Didn't keep the rumors from flying like dust in a windstorm, though. Didn't bother me, but it sure gave people something to gossip about. If you want the truth, you need to do a little investigating and stop harassing innocent people. Ol' Clive, he come after me with a shotgun and—"

"Abe, this has nothing to do with now and Egan, so please be quiet," Egan's mom said.

His grandfather bristled. "Do not tell me to be quiet. I was here long before you, missy." His grandfather and mother were not the best of friends, but tolerated each other for family harmony. His grandfather's stories were known to be long and filled with half-truths, and what he'd forgotten he made up. The older he got, the less sense his stories made.

To keep the conversation from getting out of control, Egan turned to his mother. "It's okay, Mom. I've done nothing wrong and soon the sheriff will see that."

"Egan…"

His mother wasn't having any of it. But he had to be strong this time. Being stronger than his mother might prove his biggest task. "I'm not twenty years old anymore and I'm not scared. I have to do this my way. Please understand that." He walked toward the front door and Wyatt followed.

"If you hurt my son, Wyatt Carson, I will come looking for you!" his mother shouted after them.

Wyatt tipped his hat. "Yes, ma'am."

RACHEL FLOATED IN and out of consciousness with a warm, fuzzy feeling. *Egan, don't let me float away.*

His etched-in-stone features were fuzzy. His scowl hazy. But the feeling radiating from the image in her head was comforting and made her feel secure. She'd known Egan only a couple days. Was it possible to know someone that easily and so quickly?

Her body ached and her leg burned. She moved restlessly in the bed. Where was Egan? She needed to see him. "Oh," she moaned, feeling disoriented.

"Rachel, are you awake?"

She knew that voice. It had comforted her at the most stressful time of her life. It was her best friend, Angie. Her brother's wife now.

"Angie…"

"Hey, it's good to see you. How are you feeling?"

Rachel opened her eyes. Angie was older, but she looked the same: blond hair, golden eyes and a serene facial expression that endeared her to everyone.

They hugged and Rachel held on for an extra minute. Angie was the good part about coming home. Drawing away, Rachel glanced around the sterile room. "Where am I?"

"In the hospital."

Sinking back against the pillows, she murmured, "We made it." Lethargy settled over her and her eyes felt heavy. Egan had to be in the hall and she couldn't wait to see him—to thank him. All she had to do was open her eyes, but they wouldn't cooperate.

"Rachel." Angie's voice wafted through the memory of Egan and she was helpless to respond. Something was pulling her down, down, down, and she gave in to the relaxing feeling as she drifted back to sleep.

THE DRIVE INTO town was made in complete silence. Egan was in no mood to talk and Wyatt respected his wishes. The sheriff pulled into his parking spot at the courthouse. A knot formed in Egan's stomach. He was innocent, but there was that niggling feeling that this could go very wrong.

His uncle, his mother's only brother, Gabe Garrison, who was just a year older than Egan, was waiting in the sheriff's office. He was a lawyer in Horseshoe and Egan relaxed at the sight him. His mother had made a phone call.

Gabe slapped him on the back. "Don't worry. This'll be over in no time."

Egan hoped he was right.

Wyatt was talking to Stuart, who quickly left. The

office was the same as Egan remembered: a drab outer room with three desks and filing cabinets shoved up against the wall. Wyatt's desk was situated in a corner and more private.

"What's up, Wyatt?" Gabe asked when the sheriff walked around his desk.

Wyatt picked up a pad and a couple pencils. "Let's go into the interrogation room, where we'll have more privacy."

"You don't have to say anything," Gabe told Egan.

"I have nothing to hide and want to tell my side of the story."

The interrogation room was small and claustrophobic. Egan told his story once again and Wyatt wrote it down. Every now and then he'd ask a question.

"Izzy sicced his dogs on Rachel?"

"That's what she said. I was getting water. When I returned, four dogs were on her. She beat at one with her hairbrush, which probably kept him from killing her."

"Why would Izzy do such a thing?" Wyatt asked.

"How would he know that?" Gabe interjected.

"I'm just trying to understand how this happened."

"Really, Wyatt?" Egan said. "Everybody knows Izzy's not dealing with a full deck. I was tracking dogs because they're killing our baby calves. He's trained those dogs to kill and something needs to be done."

"I'll get to that later." Wyatt doodled with the pencil. "What was Rachel doing so far from the main highway?"

"You'll have to ask her that."

The phone rang in the outer office and Wyatt got to his feet. "I have to get that. It's Sunday and I'm short on help."

"As far as I can see, we're done here." Gabe stood.

"You have nothing to hold Egan on, except the word of a man who would like to get back at the Rebels."

"Sorry, I can't let Egan go until I talk to Rachel." Wyatt hurried into the office and Egan and Gabe followed.

While Wyatt dealt with the problem, Egan glanced to the left and saw the holding cells. His life could change once again in an instant. But he wasn't going down without a fight.

Suddenly, the door flew open and Judge Hollister charged in. Egan hadn't seen the man in fourteen years, and all the anger and resentment that had built up in him rose to the surface. The man had aged. He had to be in his sixties now, with a thatch of gray hair and a scowl Egan remembered well.

Egan stood straight, his back rigid, his demeanor as serious as if a gun were being held to his head. This man would not take him down again.

Judge Hollister flung a hand at him. "Why isn't he in jail?" The question was directed at Wyatt, as he hung up the phone.

"Can I help you, Judge?" The sheriff was cool as a winter breeze.

"I'm not going to ask you again, Wyatt. Why is that man not behind bars? I presume you served the warrant."

"I'm not arresting anyone until I investigate this case further."

The judge's eyes bugged out. "Are you disobeying a judge's order?"

"No." Egan stepped forward, unable to stay quiet any longer. "You see, Wyatt has honor and integrity—unlike you."

"How dare you…"

"Oh, I dare. You like to teach people lessons, don't

you, Judge? Well, I learned a big lesson when you sent me to prison. Innocence doesn't mean a thing when you're facing a narrow-minded, bigoted judge."

"You—you…" The older man stammered and his face turned red in indignation.

Hardy came through the door. "Dad, what are you doing here? I've been trying to call you."

"What?"

"Rachel's in a hospital in Temple and we have to go. Why haven't you answered your phone?"

The judge patted the pockets of his suit jacket. "I guess I left it at the house when I took off in such a hurry. Is Rachel okay? What did he do to her?"

Hardy grasped his father's elbow and led him toward the door. "Let Wyatt do his job."

"Did you hear what that man said to me?"

"This is none of your business, Dad, so please stay out of it."

"Rachel is my daughter and you're the DA. You need to make sure Wyatt does his job like he's supposed to."

"Wyatt knows how to do this job, and neither he nor I appreciate you manipulating the system."

"Your sister was kidnapped. Doesn't that mean something to you?"

"Yes, and I'm on my way to hear her side of the story. Until then, no one is going to jail."

Knowing Hardy wasn't a clone of his father, Egan had a whole new respect for the man.

The judge grumbled as they went out the door.

Gabe looked at Wyatt. "We're done here."

Just then Ira McCray, his oldest son, Gunnar, and Izzy McCray walked in, and through the window, Egan could see trucks pulling up to the curb. The Rebels had arrived.

It was far from over.

Chapter Six

Egan's family filed in one by one, his mother in front and Grandpa and Jericho trailing behind. For some reason, that angered Egan. Years ago he had needed their support, but he was a man now and could stand on his own two feet. He didn't have time to think about it further. His mother and Ira eyed each other. Enemies, face-to-face. The tension was so thick, Egan could slice through it with his knife.

Wyatt was quick to defuse the situation. "Ira, you and your family can come in here." He held open the door to the interrogation room.

"That's him, Sheriff." Izzy pointed a finger at Egan. "He had that girl. I tried to help her, but he killed my dogs and shot at me. Lock him up. He's the one."

"You lying—"

Gunnar got in Egan's face. "Are you calling my uncle a liar?"

Egan stood toe-to-toe with him, the smell of stale peppers on Gunnar's breath turning Egan's stomach. "That, and a lot more."

"You Rebels are troublemakers."

Egan's brothers surrounded them and Gunnar moved back, as did Izzy.

"Ya gonna pay for my dogs!" Izzy shouted. "They was good hunters."

"We're not paying you a dime, Izzy, but you're going to pay for the baby calves your dogs killed on Rebel Ranch."

"Izzy's dogs are not killing your calves," Ira said.

"I tracked them to your fence line and there were no other dogs in the area. That's eight calves at five hundred dollars a head."

"You can't prove that."

"Maybe not, but now we know where the danger lies."

"Ira, I need to talk to Izzy in here." Wyatt motioned for them to come into the room, and surprisingly, the McCrays did as asked.

Kate Rebel had turned a shade of white Egan had never seen before, not even when their father died. For the first time, he realized how much his mother had aged in the past few years. He couldn't remember the last time he'd seen her smile or heard her laugh. The weight of her sons' futures and of Rebel Ranch weighed heavily upon her shoulders.

"Mom, are you okay?"

"It's just seeing the McCrays and remembering what they have done to my family."

Egan glanced at his older brother. "Falcon, take Mom home. I got this. It's my problem, my battle, and there's no need to interrupt everyone's workday."

"You heard the man." Falcon took her elbow, but she pulled away.

"Egan…"

"I got it. No help needed." His voice was strong and determined, so she'd get the message. She didn't need another worry in her life. And for once, Egan knew he could handle the McCrays any day of the week. Or anything else that came his way.

His mother glanced at Gabe.

"I'll stay on it, sis, so don't worry."

Kate Rebel followed her other sons out the door. Even Grandpa left without a word. Jericho lingered in the doorway and Egan knew he wouldn't go far. He was used to that. Somehow he'd gotten a sidekick, like Tonto in *The Lone Ranger.* But that was fictional. This was real life. That secure feeling of knowing someone was always there was the same, though.

Egan took a seat in front of the sheriff's desk and waited. He thought of Rachel and wondered how she was. Hopefully, she was okay and would have a good visit with her family if she told them the truth. He had his doubts about that.

Stuart came in and sat at his desk. "You want a cup of coffee?" he asked.

"No, thanks. I'm good."

"The sheriff talking to the McCrays?"

Egan rested an ankle across his knee and brushed dirt from his boot. "Yeah. I hope it doesn't take too long. I have work waiting for me."

"Nah. The sheriff is fast. Won't take him long to get to the truth."

Wyatt came out and went to his desk. "I'm getting conflicting stories and I really need to talk to Rachel." He picked up his phone and spoke to Hardy. Hanging up, he said, "Rachel is still out, so we keep waiting."

"Did he say how she was?" Egan asked.

Wyatt leaned forward, a gleam in his eyes. "Did you know Rachel before this incident?"

"No, not really. I was well acquainted with her father, though."

Wyatt tapped the desk. "I think we've established that."

"Can I go now?"

Wyatt shook his head. "Sorry, Egan. You have to stay here until I hear Rachel's story. That's just the way it is."

"That stinks."

"Yep, but that's the law business."

Two hours later, with still no word from Hardy, Egan knew Wyatt had to make a decision. He couldn't keep them sitting here forever. Sadly, it was not in Egan's favor. The sheriff let the McCrays go and faced him.

"Sorry, Egan, looks as if Rachel's going to be out for the night. And Judge Hollister has asked for testing to make sure the scratches on Rachel are not human. The judge doesn't buy the dog story."

Egan was flabbergasted. "What about the rabies? Isn't the man worried about rabies?"

"Rachel was immediately given rabies shots and the public health officials are at the McCray property checking the dogs. It's under control."

"I doubt if it's under control. Sounds to me like the judge is more concerned with putting me in jail than the welfare of his daughter."

Wyatt looked at his phone as if willing it to ring. "I'll admit the judge is jumping to conclusions, but he's worried about Rachel."

"So he figures I've done something to her for revenge."

"Yes, that's my guess."

"Revenge is for weak men, Wyatt. The judge will get his one day, but it won't be from me."

Wyatt stood and reached for a piece of paper. "This is a warrant signed by Judge Henley, and I have to serve it. Until Rachel can tell her side of the story, that's the way it has to be."

"Come on, Wyatt." Gabe had been on his phone and chimed in when he heard that.

"I have a warrant, Gabe. I can't ignore it."

"On the word of crazy Izzy McCray. You're getting soft, Wyatt."

The sheriff stiffened. "I've taken enough crap from the Rebels today. I'm just doing my job."

"And I'm going to do mine," Gabe said. "When Egan's story checks out, I'm going to be filing charges on a lot of people for letting a retired judge manipulate the justice system. You included, Wyatt."

Egan got to his feet before things got really heated. He surprised himself at the calmness that settled over him. Judge Hollister was not going to break his spirit— not ever again.

"Do what you have to do, Sheriff," Egan told him.

"Empty your pockets and take off your belt."

"I'm going to Temple to check on Rachel Hollister myself." Gabe headed for the door. "I don't trust the judge and his manipulations. Egan, hang in there. I'll get you out one way or another."

As the door closed, Wyatt cleared his throat and quoted, "Egan Rebel, you're under arrest for the kidnapping of Rachel Hollister. You have the right to…"

The words echoed through Egan's head. For years he'd been avoiding this, hiding out on the ranch, staying out of trouble, keeping his nose clean and avoiding people who could tempt him as they had in college. Until this moment he'd never realized what he'd been doing—avoiding life. Avoiding this situation where once again he would be placed in a cell for something he didn't do.

One thing about prison was it toughened a man. Egan wasn't shaking in his boots. His nerves were steady, because he was older and knew justice could not be blind a second time. Rachel would set him free. That might make him a little naive, but he felt he knew the woman pretty well. It was her father who gave him pause.

He removed his belt, wallet and change from his pockets and laid them on Wyatt's desk.

His boots thudded on the concrete floor as he walked to the cell. Wyatt inserted a key and opened the steel door. It clanged with a well-remembered sound that made Egan sick to his stomach, but Wyatt would never see that on his face. *Run*, was the thought blasting through his mind. But he didn't. He sat on the bottom bunk with a resignation that came from growing up.

"Again, I'm sorry, Egan," Wyatt said. "I'm going home for a little while, but I'll be back, and I'll continue to check with the hospital."

Egan nodded and scooted back on the hard mattress. As he did, he noticed Elias, who had been jailed several times for fighting, had written his name on a cinder block. Beneath it was Paxton's name. Egan felt right at home.

Wyatt turned and then swung back. "Your friend Jericho is outside. Do you think you could get him to go home?"

"Are you afraid of him, Wyatt?"

"I'm afraid of what he will do. I'd hate for something stupid to happen when all this could be straightened out in a few hours."

Egan knew Jericho would do anything to keep him from going back to prison. His friend had been there when Egan had been beaten and tormented by other inmates. If there was one thing he didn't want, it was for both of them to go through that again.

"Send him in and I'll talk to him."

Jericho came inside and stood in front of the cell door

like a big imposing wall, but half his attention was on Wyatt at his desk.

"Don't worry. I got it covered," Jericho whispered in his deep growl of a voice. "The sheriff will leave soon and I can handle Stuart. My truck is waiting outside and we can be gone in less than thirty seconds."

Egan got up and walked to his friend. "Listen to me. I didn't kidnap Rachel Hollister and I'm not breaking out of jail to risk spending the rest of my life in prison. You don't want that, either, so go home. By morning I should be there, too."

The hard-life creases on Jericho's face intensified. "I'm not leaving until you do."

"Go home, Rico. There's a load of heifers that need to go to Abilene in the morning. You're supposed to ride shotgun."

"I already told Miss Kate and Falcon that I was staying here. They said okay."

Egan looked into Jericho's eyes, and like every time he did, it was a bit of a shock. His eyes were dark, sometimes almost blank, but underneath all the darkness was a glimpse of warmth that only a few people witnessed. Egan was one of them.

"Are you my friend?"

"Till death."

"Then I want you to trust me when I say I can handle this with my eyes closed. These people can't hurt me, and if by some slim chance I'm wrong, you'll be the first person I'll ask for help. Go home, Rico. I'll call when I want you to pick me up."

He didn't move or respond.

"I'm good, man. It's just a waiting game."

Rico looked toward Wyatt, who was shuffling through

some papers. "I can get you out of here in seconds and they'll never find you."

"Come on, man, don't talk crazy."

"They'll railroad you again."

"If that happens, then you can break me out of jail. How does that sound?" There was laughter in Egan's voice, because this time he had faith in the system. He had faith in Wyatt.

Rico nodded. "I'll just hang around a little longer."

"No, Rico. You have a job on Rebel Ranch and you need to do it. Got it?"

He tipped his hat. "Got it."

Egan watched until he disappeared around the corner. He'd never had a friend like Jericho. The man would die for him. That was more than anyone needed in a lifetime. But they'd been in the trenches together. When two inmates, both at least three hundred pounds, had held Egan's head down in a toilet, Jericho had thrown them against a wall as if they weighed no more than rag dolls.

With his dark, forbidding presence, inmates feared Rico. At first Egan had, too. He'd been a skinny twenty-year-old witnessing things he'd seen only in movies. Having brothers, he knew how to fight. But he didn't know how to fight mean. Jericho had taught him that, and he'd taught him how to survive. Why he chose to be Egan's protector, Egan would never know. And Rico would never tell him. They had an understanding that went beyond anything Egan had ever experienced, even with his brothers. They'd connected at a time when they'd both desperately needed a friend.

Egan walked back to the bunk, suddenly feeling very tired.

"You know he's not leaving." Wyatt stood at the cell door.

"Yep." Egan stretched out and folded his hands behind his head. For the first time he realized he didn't have his hat. He'd lost it at the chopper and it was probably flying around somewhere on the ranch. It was his favorite hat and he'd find it just as soon as this bizarre situation was over.

"Jericho's a scary character. I never can tell if he's good or bad, and I'm not eager to find out which."

"Good idea."

"Stuart's on duty and the diner will send over supper."

Egan hadn't eaten in two days, but he wasn't hungry, just thirsty. He had to eat to maintain his strength for the next few hours, however.

"I'll be back later." Wyatt strolled to his office and soon Egan heard the front door close. Silence settled around him like a tomb, enclosing him in a six-by-eight-foot cell. He was locked in once again.

"Welcome back," he whispered to himself.

VOICES PENETRATED RACHEL'S CONSCIOUSNESS. Angie's, Hardy's and her father's. They were talking about her. She wanted to say something, but her mouth was dry and her eyelids heavy.

Another voice joined the conversation. It wasn't familiar to her and it was definitely male.

"I hated to call you here so early in the morning, but Ms. Hollister has been waking up on and off and I felt her family needed to be here. In the meantime, I'd like to share the results of the tests. I have a good idea of what happened to your daughter."

"The scratches are human, aren't they? She tried to fight off that man, but he's not going to get away with it. He's in jail and he's going to stay there."

"I'm not sure who you mean when you say 'that man.' My colleagues and I agree that the scratches on Ms. Hollister were made by the claws of a dog, several in fact. As are the bites on her neck. That's the reason we immediately gave her the rabies shots. We still haven't heard from the health department, but at this point it really doesn't matter, because we started the treatment. The infected spot on her right calf did not come from a dog. We extracted a broken-off mesquite thorn from it. Since it wasn't cleaned like the scratches and bites, it became infected."

"What do you mean, wasn't cleaned?" Hardy asked.

"The scratches were thoroughly cleaned, especially the bites on her neck, which prevented any type of infection."

"Who would do that?" her father asked.

Egan. Rachel tried to force her eyes open, and failed. Why couldn't she wake up? She twisted restlessly, fighting the drugging effect.

"Ms. Hollister, are you awake?" Rachel realized the strange male voice belonged to the doctor.

"Sweetheart, can you hear me?" her father asked.

Finally, her eyes opened and she stared at her family. She quickly searched for the one person who wasn't there. Egan. Why wasn't he here?

"Where's Egan?" She pushed the question through dry lips.

"Don't worry." Her father patted her arm. "He's not going to hurt you anymore. I made sure he was locked up."

What? She blinked, trying to understand what her father was saying, but her head throbbed and her body ached. Still, she had to focus.

"Ms. Hollister, do you feel like talking?" It was the doctor again.

"Y-yes."

"Do you know what happened to you?"

She nodded. "I got lost and then my car broke down. I didn't know what I was going to do until this very nice man showed up. He couldn't fix my car and he told me to keep walking down the road and someone would eventually find me." She swallowed. "It was getting late and I didn't want to walk alone in the dark, so I asked if he'd help me get home."

"What happened after that?" Hardy asked, and she stared into his concerned eyes.

"Hey, big brother, long time no see."

"You look terrible, do you know that?"

"Ah, jeez, kick a girl when she's down."

Hardy kissed her forehead. "We've been so worried about you. Why didn't you tell us you were coming home?"

"I wanted to surprise everyone."

"You sure did. Do you feel up to telling me everything that happened?"

"Yes, but first I'd love something to drink."

Angie poured Rachel a glass of water and handed it to her."

"Thanks." Rachel scooted up in the bed and took several sips, wincing as pain shot through her leg. Determined to tell her story, she ignored the aching. It didn't take her long to explain what had happened.

When she finished, Hardy looked at their father. "Let me get this straight. Egan Rebel rescued you, and after the dogs attacked you, he cleaned your wounds and then carried you out of there when you had a high fever."

"Yes."

"Sweetheart, are you sure about this?" Her father moved closer to the bed. "You've been through a traumatic experience."

"Yes, Daddy, I'm sure."

There was silence for a moment as her brother and father continued to exchange glances. By their lowered brows she knew something wasn't right.

She glanced toward the door. "Where's Egan? I want to thank him for saving my life."

Hardy swiped a hand through his hair. "Sis, we've had some conflicting stories."

"What kind?"

"We have a witness who said he saw Egan Rebel drag you from the car into the woods."

"What?" Startled, she coughed, then couldn't seem to stop. Once she caught her breath, she took a swallow of water and said, "You're kidding, right?"

"No."

"Who was this witness?" she asked, placing the glass on the nightstand.

"Isadore McCray."

A chilly foreboding gripped Rachel. She glanced at Hardy and then at her father. "You didn't believe him, did you?" Hardy's face paled, something Rachel rarely saw. He was always in control. "What did you do?"

"Now, sweetheart." Her father rubbed her arm again, taking over the conversation, as he was always known to do. "I was very upset and I did the only thing I could. Under the circumstances, I feared Mr. Rebel was out for revenge and had found a way to get even with me. I called Judge Henley and got a warrant for his arrest. Egan Rebel is in jail."

Chapter Seven

"What?" Rachel sat up quickly, making her head spin. She lay back and tried to calm herself. But the thought of Egan in jail was more than she could bear. She took a deep breath. "How could you do that to him again? He did nothing but help me."

"Sweetheart, we had a witness."

Her hands curled into tight fists against the sheet. "Your so-called witness sicced his dogs on me. They knocked me to the ground and would have killed me if it hadn't been for Egan. He saved my life, and for that you put him in jail. I will never forgive you."

"Rachel, I understand you're a little upset, but I was looking out for your welfare."

She ignored her father and sat up again. This time more slowly. "Let me have your phone, please," she said to Hardy.

"Sis, I'll make this right, so—"

"Give me your damn phone."

Her brother was taken aback by her tone, but he reached in his pocket and pulled out his cell. "I can take care of this," he repeated.

"You should have taken care of it from the beginning. What happened to facts? Aren't you supposed to have evidence to prove a man guilty?"

"We were worried about you."

Rachel knew they were, and most of this was her fault. Guilt was once again beating heavily upon her door and she had to take responsibility for that. She searched for Wyatt's number on Hardy's cell and touched it.

The sheriff responded immediately. "I hope you've got something, Hardy."

"Let Egan go immediately." Rachel didn't mince words. "He didn't do anything but help me. Isadore Mc-Cray's dogs attacked me."

"Rachel, it's good to hear your voice, and you've told me all I need to know. How are you?"

"I'll be fine once Egan's out of jail. What happened to justice, Wyatt?"

There was a pause on the other end and she knew the sheriff had been railroaded by her father and his cronies. So much for small-town justice.

"I'm just the sheriff, Rachel, and I have to follow the law."

"Then let Egan go. He did nothing to harm me."

"You got it."

She handed the phone back to Hardy and rested against the pillows, feeling drained. Feeling lonely. And wondering why she'd thought coming home would do her any good.

"Sweetheart…"

"Please, just leave. I'm tired." She closed her eyes.

"Egan Rebel said he would get even with me for putting him in prison, so it was natural for me to think the worst once a witness came forward. I'm not apologizing for that. I'm not apologizing for worrying about my daughter." The judge made his opinion crystal clear.

"I'm sorry I made everyone worry," Rachel murmured, opening her eyes. "And I'm really sorry an innocent man was put in jail because of me."

"Just get better so we can enjoy having you home," Hardy said. "Now, we'll leave you in peace."

The two men walked out, but Angie lingered. Until she glanced at her friend, Rachel didn't realize the doctor was still in the room.

He walked over to the bed and pushed the call button. "I'll have the nurse give you something so you can rest."

She shook her head. "I don't want any more drugs. I want to get out of here as soon as I can."

"You have an antibiotic drip that should be through tomorrow. Then I'll think about letting you go home. You still have more rabies shots to go, but you can come in for them."

Rachel snuggled down in the bed. "Thank you."

As the doctor left, Angie moved closer to her. "Can I get you anything?"

"I'd like my clothes."

"The highway patrol brought your suitcase and it's in the closet, as are your toiletries."

"Thank you."

Angie pulled over a chair and sat down. "Do you want to talk?"

"Not really."

"Erin is dying to meet her aunt. I know you go on Skype together, but she's excited out of her mind to meet you in person. She's pulling out all her art supplies so you can teach her more about painting."

"I'm dying to meet her, too, and the new addition to the family."

"Hardison Hollister III is only concerned about milk right now, and he's been a little colicky lately. I can't wait for you to see him. He looks a lot like Hardy, while Erin favors me."

"Where is he now?"

"Mavis has him. She still helps out at the house."

"I can't wait to see everyone." Rachel pulled the sheet up higher. She'd been gone so long she didn't know if she would fit into the household anymore. Just talking about family, though, made her feel better. Mavis was the housekeeper, and after Rachel's mother died, she'd been a godsend. Always there if Rachel needed her— just like Angie.

She looked at her friend. "Do you know Egan?"

"I know the Rebel family, as everyone here does. Egan's not too easy to get to know. He's more of a loner and rarely comes into town."

"I like him."

"I can see that. He's very handsome. Ruggedly so."

Rachel scooted up farther in the bed. "I...I think I love him." She could always be honest with Angie, and this time was no different. "I know that sounds crazy and I'm willing to admit it, but something in me just connected with him. Does that make sense? Does love happen that quickly?"

"I'm not an expert, but love for me happened slowly. The more time I spent with Hardy, the more I fell for him. Through all the heartache and pain that was to come, that feeling never changed. At times I thought I hated him, but that was just hurt feelings."

Rachel reached for her hand. "I'm so glad you and my brother finally got it right."

"I'm happy, Rach." Angie smiled so widely that Rachel smiled, too. Her friend's good nature was always contagious.

"I'm happy for you."

"Then why have you stayed away so long?"

Rachel looked toward the window and saw it was dark outside. She wasn't ready to talk about the past, but knew Angie would understand. "It's a long story and I'll tell you later. What time is it?"

Angie glanced at her watch. "It's a little after five in the morning and I've got to run. The baby wakes up about six for a feeding."

"Why did you come so early?"

Her friend squeezed her hand. "As Hardy told you, we've been so worried, and when the doctor called and said you'd been stirring, we came right away. We didn't want you to be here alone."

Tears stung the back of Rachel's eyes. Her family loved her, but at times it was hard to feel that love. The problem was with her, not them. The guilt had weighed her down for years and she was still feeling the pressure. When she was stronger, she would open her heart and explain her feelings to her family—just as Egan had told her to do.

"Go home," she told Angie. "I'm fine. I just need to heal."

Angie stood up and hugged her. Rachel hugged her back with all the emotion she was feeling. "I've missed you," she said.

Drawing back, her friend brushed away a tear. "I've missed you, too, and we have tons to catch up on. I'll come back later today to see when you'll be able to go home."

"Thank you."

Angie picked up her purse from the floor. "Don't be too upset with Hardy and your dad. They were just reacting to a terrible situation."

"You can't always make everything better, Angie."

In the old days her friend had worked overtime trying to keep peace, trying to make everyone smile, trying to make everyone happy. Rachel didn't need that anymore. She'd grown up and learned that life was not always happy. "You see, I've grown a backbone and can actually take care of myself these days. Although my actions lately have disproved that."

"Hardy's waiting, so I better go. We'll talk later and you can tell me about the new Rachel."

"She's still neurotic, I'm afraid."

Angie smiled as she went out the door.

Rachel leaned back and touched her hair. It was still matted with blood. She was a mess. The scratches on her arms were now a reddish blue and seemed to be healing. Looking up, she saw the IV dripping into her arm. Egan had gotten her help in time. She would be fine. But what about him? He probably never wanted to see her again.

The thought of him in jail made her sad. She wanted to do something to help him. She looked toward the window as if she could see Horseshoe, and knew that Egan didn't want or need her help. No matter how he felt about her, she would find a way to thank him for everything he had done for her.

EGAN HEARD THE front door open and immediately sat up and reached for his boots. A light was on in Wyatt's office, but everything was quiet. He sensed a presence at the cell door and looked up. The figure was unmistakable: big, strong and undeniable.

"Hey, Falcon, what are you doing here?"

"Making sure you're okay."

Egan got to his feet. "I thought you were here to break me out."

"Don't make jokes. I was worried Jericho might try something stupid, so I came in early."

"He didn't return to the ranch?"

"No. He's asleep in his truck."

"I tried, but I guess he didn't listen."

Falcon rested his forearms on the crossbars of the cell. "You've never talked much about your time in prison and I guess that's understandable. For Jericho to be so protective, it must have been pretty bad."

Egan swiped a hand through his hair and instinctively reached for his hat, which wasn't there. He felt naked without it. And vulnerable. Talking wasn't his thing, not even to his brothers. That time in his life had been shut away into a special compartment of his mind, never to be opened. With Rachel, he had opened it briefly, only because he had to.

"You know, Egan, you can tell me anything. We're brothers. We're blood."

"Yeah." His hand went to his head again. Damn, he missed his hat. "If I remember correctly, you're not one for talking, either."

"Not much," Falcon murmured, and even in the darkness Egan knew a shadow darkened his brother's eyes. A shadow known as Falcon's wife, Leah. The subject was off-limits, just as prison was. It was understood among the Rebel brothers. Sharing inner emotions wasn't for them. As that thought crossed his mind, Egan wondered why it had been so easy to share that time with Rachel.

"Another reason I came by—" Falcon coughed, then changed the subject quickly "—Gabe called last night and said that Rachel Hollister was still out. Then he phoned this morning about five and said Wyatt wanted him in his office as soon as possible. So I decided to come in and see what's going on."

"Is Mom with you?"

"Nah. I persuaded her to stay home and get the kids off to school."

"Really?" No one could persuade their mother to do anything unless she wanted to. Seeing the McCrays had upset her, Egan suspected.

"Is she okay?"

"She will be as soon as I get you home."

Suddenly, the front door banged open, lights came on and irritated voices echoed.

"Ya got this all wrong, Sheriff. I didn't do nothin'. It was that Rebel boy. He was up to no good, not me." That was Izzy's voice, and Egan listened closely.

"Ms. Hollister says differently," Wyatt replied. The sheriff opened the cell across from Egan, removed Izzy's handcuffs and escorted him inside.

The door clanged shut. "You'll be sorry, Sheriff," Izzy shouted.

Wyatt inserted his key into Egan's cell door and held it opened. "You're free to go. Rachel corroborated your story."

"Egan told you the truth, Wyatt. There was no need to lock him up." Falcon made his view clear.

"Don't start with me this morning. I've had it with the Rebels and McCrays and I'm just sorry Rachel got caught in between. I'm sorry I had to arrest Egan."

"How is Rachel?" Egan asked, walking out of the cell as a sense of relief came over him. Men were not meant to be locked in cells, even though the Horseshoe jail was downright hospitable compared to prison.

"She's doing good. They've started her on a rabies treatment and she should be able to go home soon."

That was good news. She'd been through a horrific ordeal, but that was as far as Egan's sympathies went.

He'd had enough of the Hollisters—enough to last him a lifetime.

Gabe and Hardy came through the door at the same time. Gabe looked from Egan to Wyatt. "Ms. Hollister told her side of the story?"

"Yes," Wyatt replied, placing a plastic bag holding Egan's valuables on the table. "Egan's free to go."

"This isn't over, Wyatt," Gabe told the sheriff. "The good ol' boys' network doesn't sit well with me."

Wyatt looked up. "Me, neither."

Gabe shifted into second gear for another round.

"Let it go." Egan stopped him, slipping his wallet into his back pocket. "Wyatt was doing his job. He didn't have a choice."

"That's mighty generous, considering what he put you through."

"He didn't," Egan corrected him. "Judge Hollister did." He looked pointedly at Hardy.

The man stepped forward with his hand outstretched. "Thank you for taking care of my sister. Cleaning her wounds saved her from a lot of misery. Please accept my apology for what happened."

Egan stared at Hardy's hand. He wasn't a vindictive guy, but for the life of him he couldn't reach out and shake it, accept that apology. Something was holding him back.

The phone rang and Wyatt spoke to Egan. "It's Rachel. She'd like to talk to you."

He had to make a decision, and it wasn't easy. All he wanted was peace, and the only way to achieve that was to not get involved with the Hollister family.

"I have nothing to say to the Hollisters." With that, he strolled out of the room and into the morning light. He took a deep breath, sucking in the air of freedom.

Falcon slapped him on the back. "Your partner awaits."

His brother glanced toward Jericho, leaning against his truck. "See you at the house. Mom will have breakfast ready."

Egan nodded as Falcon got into his truck. Gabe came and stood beside Egan. "I'd like to file a complaint against Judge Hollister, Judge Henley and the sheriff's department."

"Let it go," Egan said again. "Nothing good will come from that."

"If you say so. Now, I'm going home to have breakfast with my wife and Emma."

"Thanks, Gabe." Emma was his wife's half sister, and they were raising her. The little girl had stolen Gabe's heart.

"No problem."

Gabe drove away and Egan walked over to the dirty black Dodge parked at the curb. Jericho rested against it, his worn boots crossed at the ankles and his arms folded across his chest. His hat was pulled low, his ponytail hanging down the back of his chambray shirt.

Egan stopped about a foot from him. "You know, you make a lousy Tonto."

"Hmm?"

"Tonto always obeyed the Lone Ranger."

Jericho straightened. "Not when he was in danger."

Egan nodded. "Thanks, friend."

He crawled into the passenger seat of the Dodge. "Who took the heifers to Abilene?"

"Your mom called the man and said she had a crisis and would deliver them later. Nothing was getting done until you were out of that cell, and I have to agree with Miss Kate." Jericho backed away from the courthouse. "Time to get even with the good judge."

Egan fastened his seat belt. "I'm telling you like I told Gabe. We're doing nothing but running Rebel Ranch."

"He needs to learn a lesson."

"But not from me and not from you. Understand?"

"No. Someone hurts you. You get even."

"I'm asking you to let this go. Judge Hollister has enough on his plate dealing with his daughter. She'll handle the rest."

Jericho turned off Main Street. "You like this girl?"

Yeah. A lot. "She's just someone who needed help and I happened to be there. That's it."

Jericho shot him a glance. "I believe my friend has forked tongue."

Egan laughed out loud. Until that moment, he'd been spouting a lot of positive words to keep everyone's tempers in check, not knowing if he meant them. He did and it felt good not to harbor resentment. He was fine.

"Home, Tonto."

EGAN HAD A quick breakfast with his mom to assure her he was okay. Eden, Falcon's seventeen-year-old daughter, and Zane, Jude's eleven-year-old son, were rushing around getting ready for school. His brothers were already on the ranch doing their jobs. Falcon relayed everything that had happened.

"I think Gabe needs to file a complaint," his mother said.

Egan downed the rest of his coffee. "No, Mom. It's over and I'm going back to work." He kissed her cheek and made his exit before she could state her opinion again. It really was over. Why couldn't they understand that?

At his house, he found Quincy nursing a cup of coffee. "Why aren't you on the ranch?" Egan asked him.

"Just wanted to make sure you were okay."

Egan paused in the doorway to his room. "I wish everyone would stop treating me like I'm ten years old."

Quincy held up both hands. "Whoa. We're just worried about you."

Egan knew that, but he was getting tired of all the smothering. "There's a cell down at the sheriff's office that has Elias's and Paxton's names on it. I've never seen anyone worried about them when they're in jail for drinking and fighting."

Quincy got to his feet. "Because they make their own trouble and they're usually guilty as sin. You, on the other hand, had a raw deal that still sticks in our craw."

Egan was tired of fighting this battle. "I'm taking a shower and then I'm searching for my hat. I might take the rest of the day off."

"Did you tell Falcon?"

Egan unbuttoned his shirt. "No. He can figure it out on his own."

Quincy nodded. "Glad you're home, brother."

In less than ten minutes Egan was out the door. Pete jumped up and down, barking, glad to see him. He rubbed the dog's head.

"Where have you been? With the cow dogs? You know they'll eat you alive."

Pete growled and Egan headed for the barn to saddle up Gypsy.

His grandpa ambled in while he was cinching the saddle, and patted Egan's back. "Glad you're home, boy. Justice comes in all colors—the good, the bad and the very ugly. You've had your share." Grandpa eased onto a bale of hay, chewing on a toothpick. "Did I ever tell you about the time Sheriff Wilcott arrested me?"

Oh, no, not another story. Egan wasn't in the mood.

"It was back in the sixties, I think. The town council

decided no more horses in town and that got my dander up. So I rode my horse into town and tied him to the sheriff's bumper. Of course, that stupid horse crapped right there on the pavement and the sheriff escorted me to a cell. Your grandma had to come get me out, and let me tell you, I'd rather spend the rest of my life in that cell than deal with your grandma when she was in one of them moods. I called her Blue Northern because I never knew when one of them was gonna blow in. Your grandma was—"

"Gotta go, Grandpa." Egan swung into the saddle. Gypsy pranced around, ready to ride. Pete barked. He was antsy, too.

"Glad to have you home, boy. You were always my favorite."

Egan smiled as he trotted Gypsy out of the barn, Pete trailing behind. That was one of his grandpa's favorite sayings. He had said it to all of them at one time or another. His favorite seemed to be the one he was talking to at the time.

Within minutes Egan was flying through pastures, loving the feel of the horse beneath him, the fresh air on his face, even the wind tousling his hair. He was back in the saddle, doing what he did best—being a cowboy.

Thoughts of Rachel lingered. He should have spoken to her at the jail. But if he had, it would have opened a door he wanted to keep shut. She was a distant memory and he would leave it that way. Because for them there was no future. No beginning. No ending. Just nothing.

Chapter Eight

Tears ran down Rachel's cheeks and she didn't bother to brush them away. Egan didn't want to talk to her. That hurt more than she'd ever thought possible, but she understood his reaction. The Hollisters had hurt him, herself included.

She wanted to thank him, but under the circumstances it was probably best if they went their separate ways. Her mind told her that. Her heart said something entirely different. Before returning to New York, she would approach him, because leaving without seeing him wasn't an option. She'd caused him more pain and she had to apologize for that even if he never wanted to see her again.

Later that afternoon, Angie, Hardy and Erin came by. Erin was bubbly and her happiness was contagious, just as her mother's was. She talked constantly and Rachel enjoyed just watching her. As she did, she wondered what it would be like to have children. She'd never really thought about it, because her life was such a mess. Listening to Erin babble on, Rachel realized she wanted to be a mother. And she wanted her child to have dark, dark eyes.

The drugs must still be in her system, since there was no way that was ever going to happen. Not unless Egan forgave her. Not unless she fought for what she wanted. Not unless…

"Look for my hat, Pete," Egan instructed the dog.

Pete ran through bushes and around trees, sniffing the ground. When he barked, Egan followed on horseback.

His hat was hugging a big oak tree, the wind unable to dislodge it. He dismounted and picked it up. Dusty and a little mangled, it was still wearable. He straightened the brim and placed it on his head. Oh, yeah. He was back.

"Come on, boy. Let's find my rifle." He placed his foot in the stirrup and swung into the saddle again. His dad had given him that rifle when he was ten years old and he wasn't losing it. Pete trotted ahead. Egan knew where he'd left the gun, and it didn't take him long to reach that area.

When they arrived, Pete barked, sniffed and marched around the object lying in the grass as if he was guarding it. Egan dismounted, picked it up, brushed it off and shoved the gun back into the scabbard on the saddle. His father had taught him and his brothers how to care for their weapons and how to care for their horses and equipment. He'd been very rigid about teaching them responsibility.

Swinging back into the saddle, Egan felt a pain pierce his heart. It always did when he thought of his dad. He'd died too soon. His boys still needed him. But nothing could change the past. Each of his sons had accepted it and was doing his best to move on. At times, though, his boys rebelled. It was in their name. In their DNA.

Egan turned Gypsy toward the ranch and then pulled up, looking toward the hills and the cabin. When he kneed the horse, Gypsy responded, and they galloped in that direction. Why he was going back he didn't quite understand. Once they reached the wooded area, Egan slowed the horse and carefully picked his way through the rough terrain. It was after noon by the time he reached Yaupon Creek and the little cabin.

Everything was the same as he'd left it. He tied Gypsy to a post on the porch and went inside. Pete scurried in, searching for varmints. Finding none, the dog trotted outside.

On the bed was Egan's duster and Rachel's purse. The lantern was still on the floor and he put it away. Staring at his coat, he had to admit they had spent a special time here together, without the world crowding in. He had shared things with her he'd told no one.

Sinking onto the mattress, he sighed. A line from the old movie *Casablanca* filtered through his head. *Of all the gin joints in all the towns in all the world, she walks into mine.* It was exactly how he felt. Of all the ranches in all of Texas, she had to ride onto his. Was that bad luck, or what?

He ran his hands over his face and something in her purse caught his eye. The bag was big; he'd never noticed that before. It was like a small suitcase. He pulled out a sketch pad and stared. The strokes were bold and defined, clearly showing a cowboy standing on a hill looking down into a valley. He wore a dark duster and held a rifle in his hand. It was him. She'd drawn a picture of him.

Pete came inside and sniffed the pad, as if it might be something to eat.

"What do you think, boy?"

The dog barked.

"Yep, it's me. Why would she draw this?"

Pete whined.

"We don't know each other, and yet it seems as if we've known each other forever. It's crazy, isn't it?"

Pete cocked his head sideways and Egan knew he'd

reached an all-time low. He was talking to a dog as if he understood every word. Sometimes, though, Egan felt he did. That's when you knew you were a loner—when you talked to animals rather than to people.

He tucked the picture back into the purse and got to his feet. With the purse and the duster under one arm, he walked out the door, closing it behind him. And, hopefully, closing the door on the events of the past three days.

Before he started the trip to the ranch, he drank from the well and so did Pete. He led Gypsy to the creek to drink her fill. Then they started the trek home. When they reached the valley, Gypsy threw up her head, a sign she wanted to run. Egan gave her free rein and they flew across coastal pastures and spring grasses.

He pulled up when he noticed Pete wasn't with them. Looking back, he saw him lagging far behind. Egan had found Pete starving to death on the side of the road about eight years ago. He didn't know exactly how old the dog was, but he was getting up in years and tired easily. Egan waited for him to catch up.

The dog's tongue hung out and he was breathing heavily. Egan slapped his leg. "Up, boy." With the last bit of strength he had, Pete jumped into the air and Egan caught him and pulled him onto the saddle, stroking his coat. "You just wanted a ride, didn't you?"

Pete whimpered and settled against Egan across the saddle. They made their way to the ranch.

It was about seven o'clock and his brothers were finishing up for the day when they arrived. Egan followed a truck pulling a flatbed trailer loaded with fence posts and barbed wire into the big barn.

"Where did you go?" Jericho asked, crawling out of the truck.

"I had some things to do."

Elias pulled off his hat and wiped his forehead. "Only cowboy I know who lets his dog ride on his horse." He pointed a finger at Egan. "Tomorrow it's your turn to pull wire."

Egan dismounted. "No problem. Did y'all find any more dead calves?"

"No," Quincy replied. "With Izzy in jail that problem is solved."

"Don't underestimate the McCrays." Paxton joined the conversation. "They'll find some way to get even with us."

"We have to be vigilant in the next few weeks," Quincy added.

"In the morning Paxton and I are heading out to ride and rope in a rodeo in Lubbock," Phoenix told the group. "You'll be two men short."

"Since when?" Elias guffawed. "You slept most of the day and Paxton was on his phone talking up some chick."

"Don't start a fight," Quincy warned. "I'm not in the mood to break one up, and you just might kill each other."

"I can talk to a girl anytime I want, Elias. You don't tell me what to do."

Elias got in his brother's face. "Not when I'm pulling wire and you're supposed to be nailing it to a post."

Paxton's right fist connected with Elias's jaw and the fight was on. Elias came back at Pax like an angry tiger, cursing, hitting and kicking. The two rolled around on the dirt floor. Dust flew, Gypsy danced sideways and Pete barked excitedly at them.

"Stop it!" Quincy shouted, but the two kept fighting.

Egan nodded to Jericho, who reached down, grabbed the back of Paxton's shirt and yanked him to his feet. At the same time Egan got a choke hold on Elias. Paxton twisted and turned, his pearl snap shirt popping open.

But Jericho had a handful of his T-shirt in a death grip, almost choking him, and after a moment Paxton stilled.

"Let me go." Elias tried to kick back with his boots. Egan tightened his grip.

"Calm down and I will." He dug his own boots into the dirt, giving him added strength.

It took Elias a whole minute before he admitted defeat. He sagged limply and Egan released his hold. Not for a second did he believe his brother wouldn't come back at him. One thing about Elias was he never knew when to give up or when to quit. Egan kept his eyes on him.

Elias reached down and picked up his hat, slapping it against his jeans. "I'm gonna let this pass, Egan, because you've had a rough couple of days." He jammed his hat on his head. "But don't ever put me in a headlock again."

Egan stepped closer to him, his dark eyes never wavering from his brothers. "Don't threaten me. If you scare my horse one more time, I'll punch your lights out. Understood?"

Elias rubbed his jaw. "Paxton hit me and that's just asking for trouble. No one sucker punches me."

Paxton rubbed his throat and glanced at Jericho.

"You got something to say?" Jericho asked.

"Yeah, your fingers are made of steel."

"Remember that."

Paxton picked up his hat and Elias watched him. "Why are you fooling around with that girl in Horseshoe? What about Jenny?"

"Don't ask me questions, Elias, or I'll hit you again."

"Yeah, Paxton. What about Jenny?" Quincy asked, and Egan watched Quincy's facial muscles tighten. He had a soft spot for Jenny. She lived down the road, and she and Paxton has been an item since high school. But she loved paint horses and Quincy raised them. Most of her time at Rebel Ranch was spent with Quincy. Paxton was always at a rodeo somewhere.

"Not that it's anybody's business, but Jenny and I broke up again."

"And that makes what?" Phoenix rolled his eyes. "About fifty-two times."

"Shut up. It's not any of your business."

"It's my business." Phoenix jabbed a thumb at his chest. "We rope together and when your mind is somewhere else, we never place. Like that girl in Denver or the one in Cody, Wyoming. We placed out of the money because of you, so get your head straight or I'm not roping with you anymore."

Phoenix marched out of the barn and Paxton trailed after him. "Come on, Phoenix. It wasn't my fault. Those girls are always hanging around and I can't resist a pretty face."

"Or big boobs."

"Little brother, that might be a fact." Their voices faded away as they made their way to the bunkhouse. Paxton would get Phoenix to come around by the time they reached it. He was just that way. A talker. A charmer.

"I'm going to check with Mom and Falcon to see who's on the schedule to carry those heifers to Abilene tomorrow." Quincy moved toward the door.

Egan led Gypsy to another part of the barn to unsaddle her. Rico was a step behind. "Wanna go into town and get a bite to eat?"

"Nah." Egan removed the purse and duster from the saddle. Rico eyed the bag, but didn't say anything. "It belongs to Rachel Hollister. I went back and got it. My rifle and my hat, too."

"What are you gonna do with it?"

Egan looked down at the cream-and-tan purse.

"Thought I'd take it in to the sheriff. I'm sure her ID and stuff is in there."

"Why not take it to her?"

Egan undid the cinch. "I'd rather not see another Hollister."

Rico nodded. "I'll take care of Gypsy. You go ahead."

Egan always took care of his horse, but today he wanted to get into town before Wyatt left. "I owe you."

"Paid in full." Rico lifted off the saddle.

Egan strolled from the barn with the purse and duster in his hand. His truck was parked at his house and he hurried there, Pete loping at his heels.

As Egan opened the door, the dog whined pitifully. "Get in."

Pete jumped onto the driver's seat and then to the passenger side, sitting on his haunches and looking out the windshield. Egan shook his head.

The drive into Horseshoe didn't take long. He parked at the jail and let down his windows halfway. "You stay here. I'll be right back," he said to Pete.

As he went inside, Wyatt was giving Stuart orders. Evidently the sheriff was leaving for the evening.

"Egan," Wyatt said in a startled voice.

"This belongs to Rachel." He held up the purse. "She might need it."

Wyatt looked from the purse to Egan's face. "I'm sure she'd rather you returned it in person."

Egan sat the purse on Wyatt's desk, figuring that pretty much conveyed how he felt about that suggestion. He would never go onto the Hollister property. Not for any reason.

"Egan." Wyatt stopped him as he turned toward the door.

"Don't beat yourself up about what happened, Wyatt. You were doing your job. I understand that."

"I appreciate it."

Egan tipped his hat and walked out. Getting into his truck, he took a long breath and then turned the key in the ignition, just to hear a sound to block out his thoughts. But no sound could block her from his mind. He'd been trying for two days. Her lovely face was right there. In his vision he could see her gorgeous blue eyes, blond hair and sweet expression that was created to torture him. He could feel her hands on his face, taste her lips on his and breathe in the sweet scent of her. All by just closing his eyes.

Pete barked, pulling him from his reverie. Egan backed out of the parking spot and Pete kept barking.

"You are one spoiled dog, do you know that?"

Pete continued to bark excitedly and Egan made the corner turn to the Wiznowski Bakery. Pete loved apple *kolache*. Every time Egan brought the dog to town, he made a fuss about getting them. It didn't take long to buy a bagful. Egan gave Pete two on a napkin and he gobbled them up. Egan refused to let him have any more because he'd make himself sick. The rest he would offer to Quincy and Elias as a peace offering for the fight today. Elias was a sucker for sweets, just like Pete. Paxton wouldn't care. He would be in town making contact with his lady friend.

As Egan drove to the ranch, one thought was on his mind. It was over. He wouldn't have to see Rachel again. That should bring him some comfort, and he wondered why it didn't.

GOING HOME WASN'T like anything Rachel had expected. Angie and Erin made it fun and festive. A Welcome Home sign hung in the living room and colorful clumps of balloons were attached to lamps and furniture. Angie had made a special dinner and the decadent smell of pot roast permeated the house.

After her mother's death, every time Rachel entered the house, an overwhelming suffocating feeling would come over her. Today it didn't, and she realized why. It wasn't her mother's house anymore. It was now Angie's and Hardy's and their children's. New rich brown leather sofas graced the den, and Angie had blooming potted plants here and there, giving the room a homey feel. Baby things were scattered about, including a small crib.

The kitchen was basically the same, but it had that Angie feel to it, with recipe books and photos of Erin and the baby.

Rachel hugged Mavis until her arms hurt. The older woman was basically the same, except her hair was grayer.

Mavis cupped Rachel's face. "It's so good to have you home, sweet girl. It's been too long."

Rachel teared up. It had been a stressful few days and she was feeling the pressure. Seeing Mavis and the kids was making her weepy. She'd missed so much.

Mavis removed her apron. "I'm going home now, but I'll be back in the morning to help with the little one."

Rachel sat on the sofa, holding the baby. She'd never held an infant before and thought she would be nervous, but she wasn't. It was quite natural and she loved the scent of him, his chubby cheeks and the feel of him in her arms. She couldn't imagine anything more fulfilling than holding your own child. She was getting maudlin.

"What do you think, sis?" Hardy sat down beside her, tickling his son's stomach.

"I think you hit the jackpot."

Hardy glanced at Angie. "Yes, I have."

Trey made a face and let out a squeal. Angie was immediately on her feet. "I'll nurse him and put him in his crib. It won't take long and then we can have dinner."

Rachel's father was very quiet during dinner. He was probably afraid to antagonize her further because he knew her feelings about what he'd done to Egan. Erin's chatter made up for any awkwardness.

"We're getting the pool ready for the summer, Aunt Rachel. It's going to be so much fun. I wish you could stay longer."

With her arm around Erin, Rachel walked into the den. "I have to stay longer than I planned because of the rabies shots, so we have a little extra time." She had called the school to let them know what had happened, and one of the other teachers had taken over her class until she could return. It was four weeks until the end of school and Rachel had to be back by then.

Her father sat in his chair with a glass of Scotch in his hand. "Why don't you think about coming home for good?"

"I have commitments, Dad."

He waved a hand toward Erin. "Look what you're missing. We all miss you."

Rachel curled up on the end of the sofa, suddenly feeling tired. Tired of always arguing with her father. Tired of keeping a secret so deep that it continued to eat away at her. And tired of feeling guilty. She suddenly had a need to talk to Egan. It was the weirdest feeling in the world. How could that be? She barely knew him.

The ringing of the doorbell startled them. Hardy went to answer it, and Wyatt followed him back into the room. She sat up straight when she noticed her purse.

Placing it beside her, the sheriff said, "Egan dropped this by my office. He thought you might need it, with your ID and all."

She swallowed. "Why didn't he bring it himself?"

Wyatt twirled his hat in his hand. "You'll have to ask him that."

"He doesn't want to see me because of what my father has done to him." Rachel got to her feet and walked toward the stairs. "I'm going up. I'm feeling tired."

No one said anything and she was glad. She wasn't in the mood to talk. She wanted to be alone, to think about Egan. But she was unprepared for the sight of her room. Nothing had been changed in twelve years. It was still lavender and white—the room she and her mother had decorated. For a moment the sight stole her breath and that suffocating feeling came over her. She gulped in air and sat on the bed.

After a second, she opened her purse and pulled out the sketch pad. The picture was just as she had drawn it—Egan with his bold strong features. She touched it gently and held it against her chest. She had to get over him. It was just a crush—like a teenage crush. The pain went deep and she tried to control her emotions, but she had a feeling where Egan was concerned, her emotions were real and vulnerable.

How did she accept this final snub?

Chapter Nine

Rachel settled easily into living at home. Mostly because of the kids. She and Erin drew or painted almost every day. They laughed. They giggled. And acted crazy. Rachel enjoyed every second of getting to know her niece.

And then there was the baby. She could hold him forever and watch the expressions change on his face. At five weeks, he was very alert and active with his hands and his feet. Kissing his fat cheeks was her favorite pastime.

Everyone was giving her space and she appreciated that, but soon she'd have to talk to her family. It was the reason she'd come home. Every day, though, she put it off. She hated that she couldn't take that step and face all her feelings from the past.

One morning she got up early, intending to catch Hardy before he left for work. In the kitchen, she stopped short in the doorway. Her brother had Angie backed up against the refrigerator, kissing her neck.

Rachel cleared her throat. "You do have a bedroom," she quipped, heading for the Keurig.

Hardy straightened. "Just kissing my wife goodbye."

Angie tightened the belt on her robe and looked guilty. Rachel laughed. "Why couldn't you two see you were made for each other years ago?"

"I guess we weren't ready." Hardy reached for his

briefcase on the granite countertop. "Now we know what we have is real, and we both value it more than anything." He gave Angie a quick kiss and headed for the garage. "See you tonight."

"Hardy," Rachel called.

He looked back at her.

"Could we talk tonight? I mean with Dad. I have some things I need to say."

Her brother's forehead creased like a furrowed field. "Something wrong? You feeling okay? Are you upset that Isadore McCray is out on bail?"

She took a sip of her coffee to steady herself. "No." Hardy had told her earlier that a lawyer from Temple had gotten him out. That didn't bother her. The man still had to stand trial. "I'd just like to explain…how I got lost and other things. Everyone's been tiptoeing around my feelings and I would just like to air things out."

"Sure. Dad's in Austin, but he'll be back by tonight."

Rachel sat at the table and Angie joined her. Hardy stood at the door an extra second and then left.

"Do you want to talk?" Angie asked.

Rachel just wasn't ready to open up her heart, not even to Angie. She'd save all that for tonight.

Angie jumped up. "Oh, my, look at the time. I have to get Erin to school."

"What about the baby?"

"Mavis is coming over."

"I'll help," Rachel offered.

"You're very good with him."

Rachel lifted an eyebrow. "And that surprises you?"

"Yes, a little."

"I've grown up, Angie. I mean, really grown up."

"I can see that." Her friend grabbed a cup of decaf and hurried toward the door. "I'm having lunch with Peyton today. Why don't you come in to Horseshoe and join us? You'll love Peyton."

Peyton was Wyatt's wife, and she and Angie were very good friends. "Thanks, but I think I'll stay with the baby and spoil him."

"There's a lot of people in town who would like to see you."

"Not today, Ang. I have to go on Skype with my students and touch base with the school principal. Maybe another time."

"If you change your mind, the keys to your Mustang are right there. My brother, Bubba, gave it the once-over, so it's ready to go." Angie pointed to the key rack on the wall.

"Dad kept my Mustang?" She thought he would have sold it by now. A lot of good memories about the car shifted through her mind. She and her mother had found it in Austin a week before her sixteenth birthday. A white convertible Mustang with red leather inside. Rachel had loved it on sight and it wasn't long before she was driving it around town. Another memory of how her every wish was granted. She never wanted for anything, except for her mother to still be alive.

"Yes. Please think about joining us."

"You're going to be late." Rachel pointed to the clock and Angie dashed from the room. Rachel was glad for the reprieve, but tonight was the night. She was going to spill her guts, so to speak. The weight of the past and her guilt had finally gotten too heavy.

The day went well and Rachel enjoyed her nephew. Angie came home twice to nurse him. Other than that it was a quiet day, except for Trey's fussy cries. As she held the baby, Rachel rehearsed in her head what she was going to say tonight. Every time it was different and she was almost to the point of chickening out. Trey cooed at her and she knew if she wanted any type of future, she had to be honest about her feelings and be prepared to accept her family's reaction.

Erin had something at school, so Angie and Hardy were late getting home. Her father was already in his study smoking a cigar. It was almost eight o'clock when they finished dinner. Trey was asleep and Erin went to her room to do homework.

The rest of them made their way into the den. Everyone was tired and Rachel thought it would be best to wait another day. But then it would be another. And another. And she would be stuck even longer avoiding what she dreaded the most. Egan had said to just do it— and so she would.

Her father sat in his chair with a glass of Scotch. "Hardy said you wanted to talk." He started the conversation without warning and her stomach cramped.

Hardy handed Rachel a glass of wine and she gratefully accepted it. She needed something in her hands. Hardy and Angie had ice water. Angie couldn't drink because she was nursing, and Hardy did the same just to support her, which Rachel thought was lovely.

She swirled the red wine in the glass. "I know you've wondered what I was doing on Rebel Ranch."

"It has crossed my mind a time or two." Her father looked at her over the rim of his own glass.

"I don't know how to say this except just to say the words." She took a deep breath. Sensing her nervousness, Angie sat beside her for support. Rachel was grateful for that small kindness, but then that was Angie.

All she had to do was force the words from her throat, and she'd never dreamed it would be this hard. She took another deep breath.

"There's a reason I haven't been home in twelve years. I wanted to come. I missed everyone, but I couldn't handle the memories…of Mom."

"We understood that," Hardy said. "Twelve years is a long time. It's time to move on, Rachel. Mom wouldn't want you to continue to grieve like this."

Rachel gripped her hands in her lap. "It's more than that. It's…" She sucked air into her tight lungs. "I'm the reason Mom died."

A stunned silence followed her confession. The old grandfather clock chimed the half hour, blaring through the silence like a foghorn.

"What are you talking about?" her father finally asked.

"I'm the reason Mom was in the mall that day. I begged and pleaded the whole week for her to buy me a dress I'd seen for a party at school. She kept saying no and then at the last minute she must've changed her mind. She wouldn't have been there if it hadn't been for me."

The judge frowned. "Where did you get such a ridiculous idea? Your mother wasn't there just to buy your dress. We had a last-minute dinner date with the Jansons, and you know how your mom and Liz competed to see who could dress the best. She couldn't wear anything that Liz had seen, so she hurried to Austin to find something. There was nothing in the dress stores that she liked. She went to the mall as a last resort. And while she was there she picked up your dress. You're not the reason your mother died."

"What?" Rachel tried to wrap her mind around what her father was saying. "She was there to buy a dress for herself?"

"Yes, sweetheart."

Fury shot through her veins and she jumped to her feet. "Why did you never tell me this?"

"How was I to know you were thinking such thoughts?"

"By talking to me. By caring about how I felt." She ran both hands through her hair. "I can't believe this. All these years I blamed myself. I carried a load of guilt for so long that it's a part of me now, and you never took the time to tell me what Mom was doing at the mall or what she was doing in Austin. You never talked about that. Why?"

Hardy put his arm around her. "Calm down, sis."

She pushed away from him. "Calm down? Do you know what it's been like living with this?"

"No. I'm sorry."

"You're getting upset about nothing." The judge set his drink on a side table.

"Nothing?" she shouted. "It took me twelve years to get the courage to come home, and when I did, I got about five miles from Horseshoe and balked. I took the long way around and I had no idea they'd changed the county roads. I got lost. I drove and drove and felt like I was in a maze. I tried to find a house or something, but there was nothing but thick woods and more woods. I don't know what I would have done if Egan…"

"Oh, please." The judge shook his head. "I don't want to hear about Egan Rebel."

Rachel's hands curled into fists at her sides. "He deserves an apology from you." She pointed to her father. "And I deserve one, too."

The judge got to his feet, his steely blue eyes cold and unyielding. But Rachel didn't back down. "I will never apologize to Egan Rebel. He's as bad as all the outlaws out there on Rebel Ranch. He created his own reputation. I didn't."

"It means nothing to you that he helped your daughter, even when he knew I *was* your daughter?"

The judge waved a hand at Hardy. "Talk to her. She's not making any sense."

"She makes perfect sense to me," Hardy replied. "And for the record, I already apologized to Egan and he ignored me. I understood that. We jumped to conclusions and put an innocent man in jail. I don't feel good about that, and when I see him again I will continue to try and apologize to him until he accepts it."

Angie moved to put her arm around Hardy's waist.

"I wish you would've talk to me, Rachel," he said regretfully. "She was my mother, too. We could've eased each other's pain."

Some of the anger left Rachel. "I couldn't talk about it, not even to Angie. When you're seventeen and think you've killed your mother, it's a pain that goes deep. I couldn't share that horrible feeling with anyone."

"Your mother loved you," her father stated. "You were the light in her eyes and I don't understand how you got this silly notion in your head."

"Well, Dad, you and I have nothing to talk about then. Obviously, we don't understand each other."

"Now don't get your dander up. You're my daughter and I stand by you no matter what."

Rachel shook her head, wondering if she'd ever understood him. "I don't need you to stand by me. I need you to accept the feelings of a seventeen-year-old girl. And realize that you failed her."

"Now it's all my fault."

"If the boot fits, wear it." She tore out of the room and ran for the stairs.

"Rachel…"

She'd had enough for one night and she wasn't listening to anything Hardy or her father or Angie had to say. The urge to fall down on her bed and cry her eyes out was strong. But she'd outgrown that. Instead, she walked over to the window seat and curled up in the corner. That was where she'd gone when she was upset as a teenager. She could look out the window to the pool and the ranch beyond. It was always calming.

Tonight inky darkness was all she saw. Lights from the pool poked through, but she was just fine with the dark. So many times she'd sat on the seat and tried to understand why her mother had been taken so suddenly. It had always come back to Rachel's selfishness and how she was being punished for it.

Now she could see how foolish that was. It had nothing to do with her. But somehow she'd needed to feel the guilt to deal with the pain. Looking back, she realized it was the one thing that had pushed her into going to Paris to study art. She and her mother had planned the trip and Rachel had thought she couldn't go without her. Her father and Hardy had accompanied her instead, but even so she'd had to force herself every step of the way to keep going, to never look back. But the guilt was always there. She had to do it for her mother. It was what her mom had wanted for her. And now the guilt didn't even matter. It wasn't real. It was all in her head. How laughable was that?

Drawing up her knees, she found she'd never felt more lonely and couldn't wait to go back to New York. That's where she belonged. She'd carved out a life for herself with people who respected her and liked her. She was treated like an adult there, not a child.

A knock sounded at the door. "Rachel, can I come in?"

She didn't want to see anybody, but knew Hardy wasn't going to give up. "Yes."

He came inside and sat on the window seat beside her.

So big and male and out of place. She wanted to laugh, but she was far from a laughing mood.

He rubbed his hands together. "I'm sorry you've been suffering all these years. I wish we could have talked, shared more, but I don't think that's in the Hollister genes."

"It's my fault," she murmured, and realized it was. "You're right about that sharing. I didn't want anyone to know what a selfish person I was. If I kept my secret, well, then I guessed I could live with myself."

"I think we both have a lot of confused feelings about Mom's death. It was just so sudden and we didn't know how to deal with it. Our big mistake was not confiding and sharing with each other."

She rested her head against the wall. "I do believe Angie is changing you. Is she getting you to share more?"

"Yeah, with Angie it's natural. We want our kids to grow up to be well-rounded individuals who can handle anything life throws at them."

Rachel leaned over and hugged her brother. "I'm happy for you and Angie. I really am."

"I'd say I'll talk to Dad, but that would be a waste of my breath and I learned a long time ago to just let it go, for it would just wreck any kind of sanity I manage to salvage when dealing with him."

"Our father is one of a kind."

"Mmm. I'm sorry about what happened to Egan. It has put a strain on my relationship with Wyatt and I'm struggling with how to make all this right. I should've stopped it from the start and it's my fault that I didn't. I was so worried about you I made a bad decision. As the DA, I can't afford many of those."

"Egan really is a nice person, Hardy."

"You're quite taken with him."

"Yes, and I'm not afraid to admit that."

He kissed her cheek. "Get some rest. Tomorrow things will look different. Maybe you and Dad can talk again."

She gave a fake laugh. "Keep dreaming, big brother. I'm thinking about going back to New York soon. I have a job I need to return to."

"Erin will be disappointed, not to mention Angie and me. But, please, give us a few more days before you make that decision."

"I'll think about it."

Hardy left and she stared into the darkness, raising her eyes to the sky and seeing all the beautiful, twinkling stars. It reminded her of the night she and Egan had slept on the duster. She wrapped her arms around her waist, wishing he was here now. He had a straightforward way of looking at things and would understand how she was feeling. Vulnerable. Betrayed. Naive.

She uncurled from the window seat and walked around the room, trying to get rid of that feeling of despair. She'd had nothing to do with her mother's death. It was just a horrible tragedy. Her father thought she was being silly. Maybe she was. But how did she justify twelve years of her life spent in guilt and misery? By going forward.

The sketch pad caught her attention and she picked it up from the bed. Suddenly, she had to see Egan even if he didn't want to see her. Her phone was charging on her desk and she went to it. With a little searching, she found the location of Rebel Ranch. It was on the other side of Horseshoe and she could be there in probably fifteen minutes. She grabbed her purse, stuck her phone inside and crept out of the bedroom.

Tiptoeing down the stairs, she prayed no one would hear her. Though the house was dark, she found her way easily. It took a moment to locate the Mustang key on the rack, but soon she was out the door.

She had one problem, however. She had no idea where the Mustang was. After all these years, it could be anywhere. The garage was the logical place. It was connected to the house by a breezeway. Flipping on the light, she saw four vehicles: Angie's Suburban, Hardy's truck, her dad's truck and her Mustang. Oh, yes.

Sliding into the driver's seat, Rachel felt a bubble of excitement run through her. The feel of the red leather was sinful and the Mustang purred to life with a well-remembered ease, making her feel young, adventurous, even gutsy. She was reaching out to Egan and praying it wasn't a wrong decision. One she wouldn't regret later.

Chapter Ten

Egan was bone-tired and every muscle in his body ached. Working a fourteen-hour day was rough. That was a cowboy's life, though. They'd vaccinated, tagged and branded fifty-two calves, plus castrated those that needed to be. It had been a full day in the saddle and he was ready for a shower, some food and bed.

He rubbed Gypsy down. "You did good today, girl." The horse was sweaty and tired, too.

Pete barked.

"You did good, too." He reached into the pocket of his duster and handed the dog some beef jerky. Pete gobbled away, happy.

Grandpa ambled into the barn, chewing on a toothpick. "Hey, boy, where is everybody?"

Everybody had worked today, but now the ranch was quiet. "Falcon and Jude had something at school for Eden and Zane. Mom went with them and they're having dinner out. Quincy drove to Plano to check out a couple of paint horses. Jericho's in the bunkhouse, probably asleep by now, and Elias went down to Rowdy's for a beer. Someone will probably have to bail him out of jail in the morning."

Grandpa eased onto a bale of alfalfa. "That boy never met a man he didn't wanna fight."

The brothers all dealt with their father's death in different ways. Elias's was fighting.

"Seven grandsons and none of you have a wife. Now isn't that a sad state of affairs."

"Depends on how you look at it. It's not that we don't like women. We just haven't found one we want to spend the rest of our lives with." Gypsy shook her head, ready for the bridle to come off.

"Did I tell you about the first time I fell in love?"

Egan groaned inwardly. Not another story. He was too tired to listen. He made long strokes down Gypsy's wet back and didn't answer, hoping Grandpa's attention would veer in another direction. He gave it a nudge.

"Wasn't Grandma the first woman you fell in love with?"

"Who's telling this story?"

Egan shrugged and gave in to the inevitable.

"I was about sixteen when I met Wilhelmina Stugginhouser…"

"You made that up."

Grandpa winked at him. "I kid you not. That was her name. She had red hair and green eyes and was the most beautiful woman I'd ever seen. Of course, I was sixteen and hadn't seen too many. But she was a beauty."

Egan laid the brush down with a sigh. He was in for a long evening.

"She was about sixteen, too, I think, and she had eyes for me. We held hands and did a little kissy face. Back then, people married young and we wanted to tie the knot. We knew our parents wouldn't allow it so we decided to run away. Neither of us had a vehicle so we planned to walk to Temple to a justice of the peace. That woman complained about everything from her sore feet to the weather to my sour attitude. About three miles later I came to the conclusion that I didn't want to listen to that nagging woman for the rest of my life no matter how beautiful she was. About that time she came to the same decision. So we walked home and never spoke to each other again."

Egan leaned on the horse stall. "Does this story have a point?"

"Yeah, you need to find a wife and stop spending so much time alone."

"But I should walk three miles with her first?"

"What?" Grandpa's eyebrows knotted together like an old rope.

"The story. Isn't that what it meant?"

His grandfather pushed himself to his feet. "You're not gonna find a woman out there on the ranch. You should've gone into town with Elias and looked around. They don't have to be beautiful—that's what I was trying to say. Those beautiful ones are hard to get along with. Just start looking. You're not getting any younger. None of you boys are and I'm getting tired of making this speech."

If it made sense, it might be easier for them to understand. Grandpa had his own ideas and Egan and his brothers listened out of respect.

"I'm going to the house to eat the pizza that Cupcake left me and then I'm getting some shut-eye." His grandfather shuffled out of the barn, and somewhere in Egan's mind there was a voice that said he *had* met a woman on the ranch. She just turned out to be the wrong woman.

He removed the bridle from Gypsy and hung it on the wall. The horse trotted out into the corral to eat sweet feed. Egan's chaps were beginning to bother him, so he removed the duster and undid them. Laying the chaps on a rail in his spot of the barn, he froze. In the doorway stood a woman.

Rachel.

Pete barked at her. She backed away in fear.

"Down," Egan shouted, and Pete immediately sat on his haunches, staring at Rachel, just as Egan was.

Her long blond hair was loose and hung over her shoulders in glossy, tempting tresses, framing her beautiful face. Much different than the last time he'd seen her. Short white pants and a pink top clung to her curvy, feminine body. Pink sparkly sandals adorned her feet, a perfect match. The realization bounced crazily in his head.

From the sane part of his brain, he gathered his wits. "What are you doing here?"

She glanced at Pete and took a couple steps around him. "I…I wanted to talk to you."

"We don't have anything to say to each other."

"Well, then, you can just listen."

"I'd rather not."

She continued around Pete until she was about six feet from Egan. "I'm sorry you had to spend another night in jail."

"I know, Rachel. You didn't have to make a trip out here to tell me that."

Pete laid his head on his front paws and whimpered. Rachel glanced nervously at him. "Is he…?"

"He's harmless. He won't hurt you."

"I'm wary of dogs now."

Egan's eyes went to her face and arms, and he noticed that the scrapes were healing nicely. It was the fear in her eyes that was getting to him. He cleared his throat. "That will pass."

"Could we talk just for a minute?"

He heard the entreaty in her voice and he had to be

strong. Talking would solve nothing. How many times did he have to tell her that?

"I told my family my deep dark secret and turns out my father thinks I'm silly."

"What?" The word slipped out before Egan could stop it. He didn't want to know anything else about her life.

"My parents had a last-minute dinner date planned for the Saturday after my mom died, and she went shopping for an outfit for the occasion. While she was out, she picked up my dress. I wasn't the reason she went to the mall, and my father thinks it's ludicrous that I would think such a thing. Twelve years of guilt and it meant nothing to my dad. Twelve years of trying to live with it also meant nothing to him. I'm having a hard time adjusting to that. I feel as if no one understands how I felt at the time, or how I feel now."

How awful that must have been for her. Egan hadn't thought he could hate Judge Hollister any more than he did, but at that moment he harbored a new kind of hatred. What kind of person would do that to his own daughter? The worst kind. The man was an insensitive narcissist who thought the world revolved around him.

Rachel's eyes were huge and she was expecting Egan to say something to alleviate her pain. As he had so many times in the past few days, he repeated the words inside his head: *do not get involved.* It was his mantra, but seeing the sadness on her face, he found it took all his strength to remember that.

Loud howls echoed across the landscape, interrupting his thoughts. The horses in the corral neighed agitatedly. Pete barked.

Rachel moved closer to him. "What is that?"

"Sounds like a pack of wolves. We castrated bull calves today and they smell blood and are hungry."

"Are they close?"

"Too close for my peace of mind. I have to shut the barn doors before the horses come charging in."

As the words left his mouth, two fillies bounded inside, knocking Rachel against a post and galloping out the other barn door, looking for safety. Egan caught her before she fell to the ground, and sat her on a bale of hay.

"Are you okay?"

"Yes." She nodded.

"Wait here." He closed the doors before any more horses could bolt through. Grabbing his rifle from the stall, he said, "I'll be firing my gun to scare the wolves off, so don't be afraid. Come on, Pete. We have to get those horses back."

Before he pulled the other doors closed, he glanced at her one more time. Her arms were folded across her chest, as if to protect herself. She looked lost and lonely, and his heart contracted.

He slammed the door behind him.

Why did she have to walk into his life?

Again.

RACHEL TREMBLED FROM head to toe, trying not to relive that moment in the hills when the dogs had attacked her. She took a few deep breaths to calm her nerves, and looked around the barn. It was big. Stables were on the right, across from a full wall of tack. On the left side were hay bales and an open space that looked as if it held supplies. The smell of alfalfa filled her nostrils. The dirt on the floor was soft, like sawdust. To her dismay, it coated her sandals.

The howls erupted again and she forgot about her shoes. She jumped as three loud gunshots followed. The pounding of hooves sounded and a dog yapped. Then there was silence.

The barn door slid open and Egan and the dog came in. In faded Wranglers and a chambray shirt, he took her breath away. The clothes molded to his lean muscles and emphasized his strength. His boots were dusty and worn, and his hat was pulled low over his eyes. His five-o'clock shadow was sexy as hell. The whole package bespoke a hardworking cowboy. But he was a man who had stolen her heart. She couldn't explain how it had happened so quickly. She only knew it was true.

He propped his gun against a stall. "That should take care of that problem. Gunfire usually scares them away." He sat beside her on the bale and she wanted to lay her head on his shoulder, feel his strength and let him ease all the pain she was feeling.

"You're bleeding."

She glanced down at her left arm and saw a scrape on her skin where she'd hit the post. Blood trickled down to her elbow. Egan whipped out his handkerchief and dabbed at it, and she remembered the last time he'd used his handkerchief to treat her wounds.

"You should have said something."

"The wolves, the horses and the gunfire kind of had my full attention."

He held her arm and applied pressure to stop the bleeding. "I need to clean this."

"It's fine," she replied. "It's just a scratch."

He stood. "Come on, let's go to my house and I'll fix it up. This time it's my fault you're hurt."

As she got to her feet, she realized her legs were shaking, but she managed to steady herself. "You have a house?"

"I share one with my brothers Elias and Quincy, but they're out for the evening."

He took her elbow and guided her out of the barn, flipping the lights off as they went. Total darkness engulfed them, but she wasn't afraid. She was with Egan and she wasn't going to complain. Any time with him she would take. The dog followed as they walked through the moonlight.

"I noticed a lot of houses."

"There are a lot of us Rebels," he answered. "My mom, Falcon and his daughter, Jude, and his son live in the big house you passed on the way to the barn. I live in the house I grew up in, and my grandpa's house is not far from it. The bunkhouse is over by the barn."

They came to a chain-link fence and Egan opened the gate. She couldn't see much as she stepped up onto a porch. He opened the front door and they went inside. She slipped off her dusty sandals there.

The bright lights blinded her for a second. When her eyes adjusted, she realized it was a log house—a big log house. A brown leather sectional sofa with two recliners faced a big-screen TV. Another recliner sat beside it and a coffee table stood in the center of the room. Other than that, the space was bare. Through a large archway, a huge kitchen beckoned. The cabinets were a rich pine grain and the countertops were tiled in white and trimmed with hunter green. A long bar with four stools faced the cooking area. The floors had the same rich pine grain. Again, everything was plain, no-frills, with no pictures, no flowers. This was a bachelor pad.

He led her into the kitchen and she slid onto a leather barstool. From one of the cabinets he pulled out a first-aid kit. Within minutes he had cleaned the scratch and put antiseptic cream on it. He then covered it with a Band-Aid.

Unable to resist, she removed his hat, and Egan drew back, startled.

"I can't see your face."

He leaned on the bar with a twinkle in his eyes. "I think we've had this conversation before."

She met his glance with a twinkle of her own. "I believe we have."

"Are you hungry?" he asked suddenly.

"Uh…" She had already eaten, but if it meant she could spend more time with him, then she would lie.

"First, I really need to shower. I have manure, blood, sweat and no telling what else on my clothes. I'll be a few minutes." He disappeared down a hallway.

Sitting there in his home, Rachel had a warm, surreal moment. He wasn't pushing her away and she was happy about that. Walking into the living room, she thought she would like to hang paintings on the walls—paintings of horses, and maybe even cattle. It would fit this rustic home.

The dog whimpered at the door and then scratched at the screen. She didn't know what to do. Maybe he wanted inside. She'd let Egan do that, but the animal kept at it. Egan had said the dog was harmless, and she had to face her fears. She could do this. Walking to the door, she told herself that over and over. But in her mind was a horrible memory of dogs attacking, clawing and biting.

Staring down at the motley-colored ranch dog, she sucked air into her lungs and pushed the door open. The dog shot inside and trotted to the kitchen. When he didn't find Egan, he trotted back to her and barked.

"What?" she asked.

He barked again and kept barking.

"I don't know what you want."

"You don't talk Dog?" Egan asked from the doorway. He was fresh from the shower in jeans and a white T-shirt. Rubbing his hair with a towel, he said, "Pete's hungry. He wants food."

Rachel couldn't speak. She was too aware of how her body was reacting to Egan's potent maleness. Raw, primal needs ached inside her and she wanted to touch the roughness of his jaw, caress his broad shoulders and run her hands through his hair. Plus do a lot of other things with him. She'd dated. She'd had two serious boyfriends, so she wasn't a naive teenager anymore. She knew what she wanted. He was standing in front of her, all six foot plus of rugged cowboy. Who knew she liked cowboys?

While she was lost in thought, Egan opened a can of dog food and fed Pete. Afterward he pulled ham, cheese and grapes out of the refrigerator and then grabbed crackers from the pantry. He placed everything on the bar.

"Oh. What would you like to drink?"

"What do you have?"

He studied the contents of the refrigerator. "Water, milk, beer or tea."

"Tea will be fine."

She watched him eat as she sipped iced tea. "I guess you heard Izzy's out on bail."

"Yeah." Egan loaded ham and cheese onto a cracker. "Figured the McCrays would get him out until the trial."

"Mmm." She snagged a grape. "Is that all you're going to eat after a full day's work?"

Slicing a piece of cheese from the wedge of cheddar, he replied, "I don't feel like cooking and I'm not that hungry. Quincy usually has something going in the kitchen, but he's out tonight."

"So you have some sort of system here?"

"Well—" Egan popped a few grapes into his mouth

"—sort of. Quincy and I do the work and then we yell at Elias for slacking off. It seems to balance out."

They carried their tea into the living room. Pete barked at the door and Egan let him out. Rachel curled up in a corner of the sofa and he sat beside her, propping his feet on the coffee table. A lot of boot marks were visible there. Obviously, it was a habit of the Rebel men. But today Egan's feet were bare.

Rachel laughed.

"What's so funny?"

"Your feet are so white."

He wiggled his toes. "They spend most of the time in my boots."

"Have you ever been to the beach?"

He placed his tea glass on the table and rested his head against the sofa. "Sure. Lots of times, but I prefer it here."

She relaxed and for the first time today felt at peace with what had happened. She could now move forward. This house had a relaxing feel to it, as if a lot of love had been shared here. Earlier, when she'd first arrived, she'd had the feeling that Egan was going to ask her to leave. He was different now.

"Why are you not telling me to go away?"

He turned his head to look at her. "I figured you had enough for one day. What are you going to do now?"

"I'll probably go back to New York soon. I'm still dealing with a lot of resentment toward my dad, but when I think about it, I realize I jumped to all the wrong conclusions about my mother's death. Maybe because that was the only way I could deal with it at the time."

"When my dad died, I had a lot of guilty feelings, too."

"You did?" She sat up straight, eager to hear what

Egan had to say, because she knew he didn't share things lightly.

"I was in college when Falcon called and said I needed to come home. By the tone of his voice, I knew something was wrong. My dad had already passed away, but they didn't tell me until I reached the house. My mom was inconsolable and we were struggling to deal with our feelings. I kept thinking that if only I had spent more time with him, maybe he wouldn't have drunk so much. I just felt he needed me and I wasn't there. Ironically, I started to drink to kill the pain and got in with the wrong crowd. A stupid way to deal with my feelings."

She placed her hand on his forearm. "It's like we don't know what to do, so we do the worst possible thing."

His eyes met hers. "Yeah. It's time to shelve the guilty feelings. Time to move on and accept that we did our best."

She leaned over and kissed his cheek. "You smell good," she whispered.

"Irish Spring soap."

"Why are you not pushing me away?" she asked again.

"I'm too tired."

"Good. Don't think. Just feel all the good things that we know about each other."

"Rachel…"

She placed her forefinger over his lips. "You're thinking."

"Nothing can change my past."

She curled into his side. "I'm not thinking about your past. I'm thinking about now. Here. You and me. We're two consenting adults and can handle whatever happens."

"What do you want to happen?"

She raised her head and stared into his gorgeous eyes. "Call me ma'am."

His lips curved into a smile. "What do you want to happen, ma'am?"

"Make love to me, cowboy."

Chapter Eleven

"Rachel…"

"Shh." She placed her finger over his lips again. "You're thinking too much. Remember, no strings, no commitment, no fantasy, no happily-ever-after. Just us. Here and now, acting on the attraction we have for each other. You feel it. I know you do." She placed a kiss on his strong jawline, loving the roughness of his partial beard against her sensitive skin. A clean, manly scent filled her nostrils and she rained kisses all the way to his lips. Nibbling on his lower lip, she heard his swift intake of breath and then he covered her mouth with his.

She moaned and met the urgency of his lips. She slid her left knee over and straddled him. Deepening the kiss, he held her head in place. The calluses on his hands were rough, but felt like velvet to her, and she was completely lost in all the emotions that swelled within her—loving, giving and taking in the most mind-explosive way. She ran her fingers through his damp hair and pressed herself against him, wanting to get as close as possible to feel every muscle in his well-toned body.

Their tongues tasted and danced with a sense of that same urgency. It wasn't enough. He eased her top over her head and undid her bra, her breasts filling his hands. His lips teased one nipple until she wanted to scream with pleasure. With his arms around her waist, he stood, capturing her lips once again and headed for the hallway. She wrapped her legs tighter around him, her lips never leaving his. The darkness was the first thing she became aware of. There wasn't a light on in his bedroom and she didn't care. All she wanted was him. All she wanted was to be a part of him.

He gently laid her on the bed. "Just a sec." He dashed out the door and was back before she could catch her breath. "I got a condom out of Elias's room." Egan then whipped his T-shirt over his head and shed his jeans. Neither spoke as he lay beside her and took her into his arms again. Unzipping her pants, he removed them easily along with her thong. Then they were skin on skin, heart on heart and the world tilted and ceased to exist. It was just the two of them.

He kissed every inch of her body and the flame of desire blazed along every nerve ending. No one had ever kissed her like that. Completely. Caringly. Passionately. And with love. Even though he would never admit it, there was love in every touch, every caress, every kiss.

Unable to remain passive, she returned the favor, exploring his body with abandon. His muscles were tight, his skin rough and masculine. When her hand traveled across the light smattering of hair on his chest and then lower, he groaned and covered her body with his. He thrust into her and she lost all train of thought, giving herself up to the most exquisite pleasure she'd ever known. Egan's love.

It could have been seconds or minutes; she couldn't recall. All she knew was that she would remember forever this moment when she and Egan became one. He slid to the side and cradled her in his arms. Rachel lay contentedly against him and prayed that he would see that they were meant to be together.

Her tiredness claimed her and she fell into peaceful sleep, with Egan's hand on her bare stomach.

EGAN WOKE UP to a completeness he hadn't felt in a long time. Then it all came rushing back. *Rachel.* His right arm lay across her naked stomach and he immediately pulled it away.

What had he done?

He'd crossed a line and he didn't know how he was going to handle this. He'd been tired last night and had taken advantage of what she was offering. Nothing had changed in their relationship. Oh, man. He'd made a big mistake. Flashes of their lovemaking filtered across his mind and he pushed them away. He couldn't weaken.

Scooting away from her warm, tempting body, he eased from the bed and reached for his jeans. She stirred and sat up.

"Egan."

He ran both hands through his hair, searching for words, but none came to mind that would help the situation. "It's after two."

"So?" In the moonlight streaming through the window he could see her clearly, as well as the frown on her face. His gut tightened.

"Rachel, we shouldn't have…"

"Oh, please." She pushed tumbled blond hair behind her ears. "Are we back to that?"

"We should never have…"

She jumped from the bed. "Okay. I get the message." She looked around the darkened room. "Where are my damn clothes?"

"Here." He tossed her her pants and thong from the floor. "Your blouse and bra are in the other room."

She walked past him into the living room and he followed. In the lamplight, he weakened. In nothing but her pants, she was sexy and tempting and everything he had ever wanted in a woman. He wondered if he might be losing his mind, turning away from someone so perfect for him. But he had his reasons.

As she put on her bra, he looked away. Memories of touching and kissing her breasts were too vivid and real. He had to be strong.

"You said no strings, no commitment," he reminded her.

She jerked the pink top over her head. "That doesn't mean you can kick me out of your bed just as soon as it's over. That's cruel, Egan."

"Rachel…"

"Don't talk to me. I just might smack you." She looked around the room. "Where are my shoes?"

"At the door." He pointed. "You pulled them off when you came in."

She slid her feet into them and Pete scratched at the door. With one hand, she opened it, and Pete scurried outside. She went through the door before it closed.

"Rachel…" Egan followed her out onto the porch.

She swung around, her blue eyes blazing. "Don't say my name. You don't have the right to say my name."

"There is no future for us. Can't you see that?"

"I didn't ask for a future. All I asked for was a lover. A kind one who would consider my feelings."

"You want more than that and you know it."

"I leave for New York on Monday or Tuesday, and I'm not sure how much more you think I want, because I know you're not coming with me."

"You're not a one-night stand."

"That's an excuse, Egan. You're scared. You're scared of what you're really feeling, and you're pushing me away because that's all you can do right now. But I deserved more."

"Your father is Hardison Hollister and that ends any kind of relationship we could have. I can't tolerate the man and I refuse to be around him."

"Yes, I've heard the story." She looked off into the night. "Stay out here in your safe little world where no one can touch you. Where you're free without the every-day hardships of life. Without the rewards of love and your own family. Stay here, Egan, because that's what you really want. You're scared to attempt anything else, and that surprises me because you're the strongest man I've ever known." She took a deep breath. "Thank you for saving my life."

With those words she walked into the darkness toward her car, leaving him feeling empty and alone. And scared, just as she'd said. How could a grown man be scared to live? To accept love?

The Mustang revved up and drove off into the night. A piercing pain shot through Egan and he knew he'd just lost something precious. Something he should fight for.

Pete barked at his feet.

"Yeah, boy, I might regret that for the rest of my life."

EGAN TOSSED AND TURNED until five, and then he got up, made coffee and fixed breakfast. With little sleep, he knew the day was going to be a long one. But he was re-vitalized in other ways: his mind was clear, his muscles relaxed and he wasn't so edgy.

Pete growled and Egan fed him another piece of bacon.

"You know, I don't think you're getting old. You're just fat and lazy."

A blonde came from the hallway, wearing a rumpled red dress and carrying red high heels in her hand. She made a dash for the back door. "You haven't seen me," she said.

"O-kay." Egan knew the woman. She was the daughter of the owner of Rowdy's. She and Elias had come in about 2:30 a.m. Giggles and moans had interrupted what little sleep Egan had managed to get.

As he poured another cup of coffee, Quincy came in the back door with a duffel bag in his hand. "Was that Tammy Jo Snyder just leaving?" he asked.

"Yep."

"What was she doing here?"

Egan sat at the table to nurse his coffee. "Elias." He didn't need to say anything else.

Quincy shook his head and went to his room. In a few minutes he was back for a cup of coffee. Jude walked in about the same time. Tall and lean, Jude favored Egan more than any of the other brothers. They had the same dark eyes, too. Jude was known as the quiet, responsible one. He didn't talk much.

He grabbed a mug. "Falcon wants to brand and work the calves in the northeast pasture. That's close to the Mc-Cray property line and Mom doesn't want any trouble."

"We can handle that." Quincy filled a plate with scrambled eggs and bacon that Egan had cooked.

Before the discussion went any further, Elias stumbled into the room, butt naked.

"Did you forget something?" Quincy asked.

"What?" Elias's eyes were bloodshot and he looked disoriented. He had a hangover—big time.

"Your damn clothes," Jude said. "Unless you plan on riding like that."

Elias looked down. "Hell. Where's my underwear?"

"That's what we were wondering," Egan answered.

Elias stumbled back to his bedroom and returned in a pair of jeans. "I need coffee. Bad."

Jude moved away from the coffeepot. "When are you gonna get your act together? Partying all weekend is one thing, but now you're doing it during the week. It's time to grow up. It takes all of us to run this ranch."

"Well, at least I don't live with my mama."

That's when Jude coldcocked him right in the nose without spilling a drop of his coffee. Elias went flying backward onto the linoleum and lay there like a dead rat.

It was hard to say who was more shocked, Jude, Elias, Quincy or Egan. Jude wasn't known for violence. He rarely fought with his brothers, and for him to hit Elias, something had to be bothering him. But then, maybe it took all these years to lose his temper, because everybody at one time or another wanted to hit Elias.

Jude placed his cup on the counter and walked out. Quincy squatted by Elias.

"What are you using for brains these days?"

Egan squatted on the other side. "Obviously, not what the good Lord gave him."

Elias blinked his eyes several times. "Are there birds in here?"

"No," Egan replied.

"I hear chirping."

"It's your brains leaking." Quincy reached down and grabbed one arm, and Egan took the other. They pulled him to his feet.

"Did Jude just hit me?" Elias wiped the blood dripping

from his nose with the back of his hand. Egan quickly handed him some paper towels.

"Yeah," Quincy told him. "And if I were you, I wouldn't make that same crass remark to Falcon, because you might not wake up for about three days, and maybe not then."

Elias held his head back to stop the bleeding. "Why is everyone so sensitive?"

"Go take a shower and get dressed." Quincy gave him a push toward the bathroom. "And no back talk."

After Elias disappeared, Egan asked, "What's up with Jude?"

"Paige's sister is in town paying taxes on the old home place. She was seen at the bakery talking to people who Jude knows."

"And he's worried someone might tell the sister about Zane?"

"That's about it."

"Is she still in town?"

"I don't know and I'm not asking. Let's go to work."

Egan put the cups in the sink and followed his brother out the door. Just like Leah and Falcon, Jude and Paige had been lovers in high school. Paige was an incredibly smart young woman and valedictorian of her class. She'd received a full scholarship for medical school and was devastated when she found out she was pregnant. After she and Jude talked about it, they'd decided to give the baby up for adoption. But Jude couldn't live with that decision. He went back to the clinic and got his son and raised him. To this day Paige didn't know that. And Jude never wanted her to find out. Paige's family had moved away from Horseshoe, but the old house was still here and owned by Paige's mother.

Thinking about someone else's problems was better

than thinking about his own. Egan wasn't sure how last night had gotten so out of control. Putting it out of his mind was not an easy thing to do. The touch of Rachel's hand, the feel of her skin and the caress of her lips was strong, and he couldn't shake it. But he would.

He tightened the cinch on Gypsy. Rico strolled in and stared at him.

"What?"

"I heard wolves last night and came back to the barn to check on you, and you were with a woman. A pretty blonde."

For Jericho to mention this, Egan knew he had to be concerned about him.

"It was Rachel Hollister. She wanted to say thank-you."

Rico nodded, but there was no relief on his face.

"Now what?"

Rico shrugged. "Nothing."

Egan laid an arm across his saddle. "You saw us go to the house?"

"None of my business, man."

"You're the best friend I've ever had, Jericho. Even my friends in high school deserted me when I went to prison. But you're a friend for life and I can tell you anything. Ms. Hollister was here last night to thank me and things got a little heavy. No worry, though. She won't be coming back."

"Do you want her to come back?"

"What?" Egan checked to make sure everything was tight on the saddle, and lost his train of thought.

Before he could gather his wits, his mom and Falcon walked into the barn. Quincy and Jude, followed by Elias, came in from the other end leading their horses, ready for work.

"Good, everyone is here." His mom, dressed in a

printed chambray shirt, jeans and boots, started the conversation. An old worn straw hat rested on her head. She always looked the same, except Egan now noticed the worry lines etched on her aging face. "We're going to work the calves in the northeast pasture next to the McCray property. I want you to have your eyes and ears open. I don't want any trouble, but I don't want you to run from it, either. Since the dog incident, the McCrays are going to find a way to get even. They always do."

Quincy swung into the saddle. "We got it covered, Mom. Don't worry."

Egan led Gypsy out of the stall.

"Egan, I'd like a word with you."

He stilled. It was almost as if she knew.

"Is it important? It's a long ride and we need to get started."

"It'll only take a minute." His mother walked out of the barn and he had no recourse but to follow. He felt as if he was six years old and had broken the window in Grandpa's house. "I'd like a word with you" was a saying she used that always meant trouble.

She got right to the point. "When we returned last night, there was a white car parked at the barn. Since you were the only one home other than your grandpa and Jericho, I'm assuming someone came to see you."

"Yes." He wasn't going to be grilled.

Her dark eyes stared into his and the memory of her coming to see him in the prison, with that shattered look on her face, suddenly hit him in the chest like a balled fist. He never again wanted to see her wearing that expression.

"It was Rachel Hollister." She probably already knew that, but he wasn't going to lie. He'd outgrown that a long time ago.

She shook her head. "Son, please don't get involved with the Hollisters."

"You don't have to worry. Ms. Hollister came to say thank-you and she won't be coming back."

His mom reached up and patted his cheek. "She knows a good thing when she sees it, but my handsome son is not for her."

The urge to say a lot of things was strong, but he took the high road. There was no need to point out that he was over the age of twenty-one and could choose any woman he wanted. It wasn't for her to approve. He'd hurt his mother once deeply and he would never do that again.

He reached down and kissed her cheek, which he didn't do often enough. "Have a good day."

He marched back into the barn, saddled up and rode out to join his brothers. Everyone was telling him Rachel was bad for him, and he had told himself the same. But a part of him denied it. Rachel awoke something good in him that evoked thoughts of love, home and family.

When Egan kneed Gypsy, she shot off like a bullet and visions of Rachel faded, the way they should. The way it had to be.

RACHEL WOKE UP with a tear on her cheek. She brushed it away and crawled out of bed, shocked to see it was ten o'clock in the morning. After the passion of last night, and then the heartbreak, she'd been exhausted and had overslept. The house was quiet, so she figured everyone must have left for the day, which was good. She didn't want to talk to anyone.

Sinking back onto the bed, Rachel found that memories of last night refused to go away. She'd told Egan no strings, no commitment, and she'd meant that. It was his callousness afterward that got her. She didn't expect him to be so cold and irrational. And it hurt more than she wanted to admit. Waking up in his arms to find a smile on his face would have cured a lot of her heartache.

She wrapped her arms around her waist. Their love-making was everything she'd wanted it to be. He was gentle, considerate and passionate. He'd made her forget everything but him, and there had been nothing between them but the explosive emotions they shared. It was later, when their minds cleared, that the problem started again. Or she should say *his* problem started again. Her father, and Egan's involvement with him. That would always be between them, no matter how much she loved him or how hard they tried to build a relationship. She'd tried not to believe it, but now she did.

It was very rare that she lost her temper, and last night she had said things she would regret. Rachel got up and headed for the bathroom. It was just as well. There was no future for her and Egan, and it was time for her to accept that and move on. She would check on flights today and make plans to return to New York. That's where she belonged. Not in Horseshoe, Texas, with Egan.

Chapter Twelve

Rachel showered and changed and hurried downstairs. Her cell phone beeped and she stopped on the stairs to fish it out of her purse. It was a text from Angie: The baby had a doctor's appointment this morning so we had to leave early. Please try to come in for lunch. Let me know.

She texted back: I'll try. I have to get my rabies shot first. I'll text later.

In the kitchen, Rachel stopped short. Her father sat at the table reading the *Austin American-Statesman* newspaper and sipping coffee. Mavis was wiping the counter.

Seeing Rachel, she said, "I have things to do upstairs." She gave her a hug as she passed.

Her father looked up. "Morning, sweetheart."

"Morning, Dad." Slipping a K-Cup of French Vanilla in the Keurig, she mentally braced herself, wondering what to say to him. So many emotions churned inside her: anger, disappointment and oddly, love. She loved her father and she wasn't going to try and deny that.

Gripping the warm cup, she turned to face him. For the first time she noticed how much he had aged in the past twelve years. His hair was now completely gray and the lines around his eyes were more pronounced. Her mother's death had hit him hard. It was easy now to see

Rachel wasn't the only one who had been affected by her mother's passing.

Her father folded the paper and pushed it aside. "Sweetheart, it's good to have you home. I don't think I've said that. There seems to be so much going on and emotions erupting at every turn. I want to apologize for my reaction last night. I had no right to act as if your feelings were silly. I'm sorry for my insensitivity. But the thought that you lived with this enormous guilt hurts me deeply. Even if your mother had gone to that mall specifically to buy your dress, you still wouldn't have been the cause of her death. No one but those hoodlums were responsible."

Unable to stop them, Rachel found tears filling her eyes. Her father rarely apologized and he'd chosen the perfect time to do so. She needed to hear his words. "Thank you, Dad. I don't know—" she brushed away a tear "—why I felt that way, but now I feel liberated. I probably should've seen a therapist at the time, because I had so many conflicting doubts and emotions. But twelve years and I've come full circle. It's time for me to move on and live my life. I plan to return to New York, probably next week. I'm glad we had this time to say we're sorry."

He reached out for her hand and she gripped his tightly. "I wish I could persuade you to stay a little longer. Erin adores you, and Angie and Hardy are so happy to have you here. I am, too. But I understand your need to live your own life. I just hope you come home to visit often now. We are your family."

Fighting more tears, she hugged him. Really hugged him, as she should have that day in the hospital. "I love you, Daddy, and I promise to come home as often as I can."

Later, as she got in her car and drove toward Temple,

she felt lighter. Happier. Even with Egan's rejection still strong on her mind, she'd made the right decision to return to New York. Patching things up with her father meant a lot. He hadn't mentioned Egan and she didn't see the need to bring him up. Egan was now in her past. It hurt to even think it, but she would get over him. She didn't have much choice.

Her thoughts wandered as the Texas scenery flashed by. When she was a kid and a teenager, she'd felt her father could solve all her problems. She was his little princess and her wish was his command. It took losing her mother for Rachel to realize that the world wasn't like that. Wishes weren't granted automatically. They had to be earned, and even though her father paid a lot of her bills, she tried to stand on her own two feet and be responsible. Sometimes he made that hard because he didn't want her to do without. They probably needed to have another talk about that. Above all else, she wanted to be independent.

It took longer than she'd expected to get the shot, and then the doctor wanted to talk to her. They had to set up an appointment at a clinic in New York. That took time and she missed her lunch with Angie. It was almost three o'clock when she circled the courthouse looking for a parking spot near the bakery. There was none. The bakery was the busiest spot in town. She parked at the courthouse, hoping Wyatt wouldn't give her a ticket. The people of Horseshoe still parked at the curb and there wasn't a No Parking sign.

She got out and looked around the small town where she'd grown up. The courthouse sat in the middle of the square, with businesses situated around it on Main Street. Nothing much had changed. The courthouse stone was still weatherworn, showing the passage of time. The crape myrtles added color and the large oak trees provided shade for residents who gathered on the benches beneath them to visit or share a gossip or two.

More antiques shops had opened, plus a tearoom and a Mexican restaurant. Horseshoe went along at a slow pace, so different from her busy life in New York. She was always on the run, trying to catch a cab, to make it to school on time or just keep up with the hectic lifestyle. Here everyone knew each other. In New York, Rachel didn't even know her next-door neighbors. She said hello when she saw them, but other than that, no one was that friendly. And everyone minded their own business. In Horseshoe everyone knew each other's business and it caused more than a few rifts. The lifestyles were so different: country versus city. Rachel had never been sure where she fit in, but now she did. She didn't belong in Horseshoe anymore. And it had nothing to do with Egan.

She didn't bother to lock her car. People felt safe here and that was a plus for living in a small town. She hitched her purse over her shoulder and headed across the street to Angie's office. The Wiznowski bakery had expanded and Angie now had her accounting office attached, with its own private entrance.

"Rachel."

She turned to see a tall man wearing a Stetson coming toward her. She didn't recognize him at first until she saw the badge. The sheriff, Wyatt Carson.

Crap! Was he going to give her a ticket?

"Hey, Rachel, it's good to see you in town." They shook hands. "You look great. I'm glad you have no aftereffects from the attack."

The night he'd returned her purse, she'd been so upset that Egan hadn't brought it that she hadn't paid much attention to Wyatt. He basically looked the same: tall, broad shouldered and handsome. He'd sent a lot of female hearts aflutter over the years, but to Rachel he was always her big brother's friend.

"Thank you."

He motioned toward Angie's. "Are you headed that way?"

"Yeah."

"Me, too."

They fell into step as they crossed the street. "I have to pick up my son from Peyton, my wife. She has to help our daughter, Jody, for something at school. Peyton is better at that than I am. I have two kids now, you know."

"Yes, I heard. You and Hardy are keeping Horseshoe populated."

"We do our best, ma'am."

Her heart took a nosedive at the word *ma'am*. Wyatt didn't say it like Egan did, and for a moment she stood there, completely still, wondering how that one little word could be so important to her and make her heart utterly stop.

As if sensing her thoughts, Wyatt said, "I'm sorry about what happened to Egan. I know you were, too."

Rachel blinked, trying to focus on the conversation. "Yes…yes. I was. But you should say that to Egan."

"I have, and he was a good sport about everything."

"That sounds like Egan. He—" She immediately stopped what she was going to say because she knew it would reveal too much of what she was feeling. "I'm just sorry my father had to get involved."

Wyatt nodded. "Hopefully, for the last time."

He opened the door and they walked into Angie's office

"Dad-dy. Dad-dy." A little brown-haired boy, about

two, ran to him and wrapped himself around his leg. Wyatt lifted him into his arms.

"This is J.W., otherwise known as the boss of the family," Wyatt said, introducing his son. A blonde who had been talking to Angie walked over. Wyatt slipped an arm around her waist. "And this is my wife, Peyton."

"Nice to meet you." They shook hands. "I've heard so much about you from Angie," Peyton said.

"Likewise. Angie and I have known each other forever."

"We have to do lunch or something—"

"Dad-dy," the little boy interrupted.

"He's been waiting and waiting for you." Peyton brushed back their son's hair. "And I have to get going or Jody will be upset."

They quickly said their goodbyes and the Carsons left. Rachel looked around the spacious office with terra-cotta walls, plants and photos of the kids. All Angie.

"Looks nice."

"It's so good to be away from the bakery, although it's only a few steps through that door." She pointed and then walked over to the crib beside her desk. "He's been sleeping for a while and everyone wants to pick him up. I'm fiercely guarding him or I'll be up all night."

AnaMarie, Angie's older sister, came in, with a big white apron covering her slacks and blouse. A net covered her brown hair. AnaMarie did most of the baking now, Angie had said. "Is he—Rachel!" She grabbed her in a big hug. "Look at you. All sophisticated, but then you always were."

Before Rachel could respond, Doris, their mother, walked in, dressed similarly to AnaMarie. "Rachel!" Doris pulled her into her ample bosom and Rachel caught a whiff of vanilla. It was like coming home. "What do you think of our Erin? Isn't she something?"

"I adore her." Rachel knew Doris hadn't been happy when she'd found out Hardy was Erin's father, but she'd clearly adjusted.

"And now another baby in the family. My heart is full."

Angie's twin sisters, Patsy and Peggy, the beauticians, came through the front door and there were more hugs and laughs. The twins could always make Rachel laugh.

"Look at her beautiful hair," AnaMarie said to the twins. "Why can't you do my hair like that?"

"It's like a canvas, big sis," Patsy told her. "You need something to work with first, and that mop of yours is like straw."

"Shut up."

"You shut up."

Peggy put an arm around Rachel. "Don't listen to them. I could put a streak of purple in your hair that would be dazzling."

"Leave the girl alone," Doris said. "She looks fine without you messing with her hair. You could use less purple."

Peggy flipped back her blondish-purple hair. "You have no taste."

"Enough," Angie interrupted. "If you wake the baby, I will throttle all of you."

"That's what we were trying to do," Patsy said with a laugh. "We rarely get to hold him because Hardy has all these rules. He's like a wart on my butt. Annoying."

"There are rules because if we hold him all day, he wants to be held all night, and Hardy and I are the ones who have to be up with him." Angie looked at the clock on the wall. "In about thirty minutes he'll awake for a feeding and then everyone can hold him. After that, I'm going home to my family."

"See how she's gotten." Patsy nodded to Rachel. "Bossy and annoying just like her husband."

It was always fun to be around the Wiznowski sisters. They had a sort of no-holds-barred relationship with each other: honest and straightforward, even when it hurt. Life was simple in Horseshoe. A part of Rachel wanted the life and happiness she'd had when she was a kid. But that was just because the memories were so good. Until her mother's death.

Angie shook her head as her sisters and mom went back to work. "It's like a day at the zoo."

"But it's nice to have family around. I love New York, but it gets lonely sometimes."

"Then come home. This is where you belong."

Rachel was searching for an answer when the door opened again and a pretty blonde walked in. Rachel didn't recognize her. Angie fidgeted with papers on her desk and Rachel knew this woman had some sort of significance, to make Angie nervous.

"How did the appointment go?" the blonde woman asked. She tiptoed to the crib and Angie got up to join her.

"Everything was fine. The doctor said he's right on schedule."

"He's so adorable and I just want to pick him up and smooch him."

"His cheeks are so kissable," Rachel said without thinking.

The blonde looked at her. "Oh, I don't think we've met. I'm Lacey Garrison and I own the flower shop two doors down."

"I'm Rachel Hollister. It's nice to meet you." Obviously, the woman was a friend of Angie's, but then everyone was a friend of Angie's.

"Oh." Clearly, the woman was startled.

"Rachel," Angie hastened to explain, "Lacey's husband is Egan's uncle."

"Oh." This time Rachel was the one stunned.

"I'm so glad you're okay," Lacey said. "After what you've been through, you look great."

"I'm so sorry about what happened to Egan."

"We all were, and Gabe did everything he could to keep him out of jail. If you remember a tall, sinfully good-looking man in your hospital room, that would be my husband. He wanted to get the truth as soon as possible and he wasn't trusting anyone."

"I was out most of the time, but I'm glad he was there to help Egan."

Lacey glanced at her watch. "I've got to run." She looked at Angie. "Do you need me to pick up Erin?"

"She has something at school and Hardy will pick her up later. But thanks."

"No problem. You've helped me a million times." Lacey's eyes settled on Rachel. "I hope you enjoy your stay in Horseshoe. It has become my favorite place in the world."

"Thank you." Rachel liked the woman and wanted to say more. "I would like the Rebel family to know how grateful I am to Egan for saving my life. He will always have a special place in my heart."

"Egan is kind of special, but then I'm partial to the Rebels. Nice meeting you."

After the door closed on Lacey, Rachel turned to Angie, who was making sure Trey was covered up. "I like her."

Angie walked back to her desk. "Yes. She's had a rough year, but we've all tried to be there for her."

Rachel sank into the leather chair across from her. "What happened?"

"Her father passed away and left her guardianship of her six-year-old half sister. Gabe was her next-door neighbor and had lost his eight-year-old son in an accident. They both were struggling and we all were so happy when they found love…with each other."

"Maybe dreams come true in Horseshoe, Texas."

"Which reminds me." Angie leaned back with a smug expression on her face. "Last night as I was going to bed I heard a sound and looked out the window, to see lights going down the road. It had to be you, so my question is where did you go that late at night?" She held up a hand as Rachel started to speak. "And don't say it's none of my business. I love you and I worry about you, especially since you shared your reasons for not coming home for so long."

Rachel ran her hands through her hair. "You probably know where I went." She didn't see a need to lie.

"You went to visit Egan?"

Rachel nodded as tears formed at the back of her eyes. She hated that she was this weak.

"From your expression, I'd say it didn't go well."

Rachel was used to sharing things with Angie, except her deep dark secret about her mother. Maybe Egan should be one of those secrets. But she needed to talk to someone.

"I went to thank him for what he did for me, and it went really well. We had one of those evenings I'll never forget. He was loving, kind and caring. Everything you want in a man."

"So what happened?"

She swallowed. "Afterward, he make sure I knew there was no room in his life for me."

"Why?" Angie asked softly.

"Be-because of what my father did to him. There's just no getting around that. In a way, I understand it, but if what we were feeling was real, it wouldn't make a difference."

Angie got up, came around the desk and hugged her. "I'm sorry, Rach. I know how you feel about him, but give it some time. You've only known him a week."

"Yeah. I'll be the first to admit that my emotions aren't exactly stable right now."

"Let's have a girls' night out tonight. Hardy's taking Erin out to eat, to give her some extra attention. Everyone just wants to hug or hold the baby. They seem to forget about her, and Hardy and I don't want to make that mistake. She loves time alone with her dad."

"Sounds good. I'll be leaving Horseshoe as soon as I get a plane ticket. Maybe Monday or Tuesday."

Angie's face fell. "Oh, Rachel. I was hoping you'd stay longer."

"I have a job to get back to."

The baby made a fussy sound and Angie's attention was instantly diverted. It was just as well. Angie couldn't talk her out of her decision. On cue, Doris and AnaMarie came charging in as if they had an extrasensory perception to baby sounds. Laughter ensued as they argued who was going to hold him first. Rachel left Angie to sort out the problem; she'd been dealing with her lively family for years.

Rachel walked across the street and got into the Mustang. She sat for a moment staring at the timeless courthouse. Memories flooded through her mind. So many times her mother had brought her here to visit her dad.

She'd sit in his big chair and pretend she was a judge. When she grew older, she still would sit in his chair, but she didn't pretend so much.

Even as a little boy, Hardy had always known he wanted to be a lawyer and to follow in his dad's footsteps. Since Rachel drew pictures and loved to paint, everyone had assumed she wanted to be an artist. It was never her decision. It had been made for her by her mother and father.

She turned the key and the engine fired to life. Backing out, she thought it was time for her to decide what she wanted to be for the rest of her life. She loved teaching kids and she loved her job in New York, but it was all about the kids—their funny faces, their sweet smells, naïveté and innocence. Just being around their enthusiasm filled her with joy.

Turning off Main Street, she knew exactly what she wanted to be for the rest of her life: a wife and a mother.

Chapter Thirteen

"Yee haw," Elias shouted, and kneed his horse. "Later, suckers." Off to the barn they flew.

Falcon shook his head. "That boy doesn't have a lick of sense."

Egan agreed with his older brother. Elias had slid off his horse three times today because he'd fallen asleep. His head had to be made of something similar to a helmet, because he kept taking hits and getting back up.

The other brothers followed more slowly. It had been a long day and everyone was tired and ready for rest and food. They hadn't had any problems with the McCrays today. Gunnar had ridden the fence line several times, but made no move to interact with the Rebels. They'd done their job and ignored him.

Their mother had driven the ranger out at noon with lunch and Grandpa had followed on his horse. Egan knew his mother was worried, and that she was keeping a close eye on everything. Grandpa was the entertainment, regaling them with his stories.

They rode into the barn to their respective stalls and unsaddled the horses. Elias lay sprawled on bales of alfalfa.

Grandpa poked him. "Get up from there. What's

wrong with you, boy? You know you always take care of your horse first."

"Ah, I need a minute."

Grandpa sat beside him and Elias groaned. "You're getting too old to be partying during the week," the old man said.

Elias raised his head. "I'm only thirty-three."

"Did I tell you boys about the time I didn't sleep for a week?"

"Ah, Grandpa, my head hurts enough."

"It must've been about 1960 or so. Your father was small."

Egan's chest tightened at the mention of his dad, as it always did. And he knew his brothers were feeling the same. Talking about their father wasn't easy.

"It was about this time of the year, too. I was busy baling hay and your grandma was run off her feet canning stuff out of the garden and helping me when she could. Her sister, Ruth, came to help. One night I worked till after dark getting hay into the barn, and I was tired as an old hound dog who'd been hunting all night. I wasn't even hungry. I just went to bed. Around midnight I heard screaming and it woke me right up. Lights came on and I didn't know what the hell was going on. But your grandma stood in the doorway with fire and brimstone in her eyes. About that time I realized I was in bed with Ruth. I was so tired I'd gotten into the wrong bed. I tried to explain, but your grandma wasn't listening. She locked me out of the house. I tried sleeping on the porch, in the yard, in the barn, but I just couldn't sleep without Martha. And she wasn't listening to one word I had to say."

"What made her let you back in the house?" Elias asked, and everyone waited for his answer.

"Now your grandma was a petite, pretty little thing,

and Ruth looked like a linebacker for the Dallas Cowboys. I told her if I was gonna sleep with somebody else, I'd pick one of them big-boobed barmaids at the beer joint. I certainly wouldn't pick Ruth."

"And she bought that?"

Grandpa frowned so deeply the grooves in his forehead looked like ruts. "What are you talking about? I was telling the truth, but the big-boobed remark got me another night in the barn. Women." He shook his head. "I'll never understand them, but I sure loved your grandma."

Egan led Gypsy into the corral to the feed trough. His dad had loved one woman and so had Grandpa. Rebel men tended to love once and deeply. But it took a lot of patience on the woman's side. Grandma Martha had been a warm, loving person and Egan remembered her well. She had a temper, too, and Grandpa had steered clear of it, even though he'd been the cause of it most of the time.

With the horses unsaddled and taken care of, the brothers started toward their homes, along with Jericho.

"Quincy, you coming to my house?" Grandpa asked. "Cupcake's got something at school."

Everyone was tired and Egan saw the expression on Quincy's face. He just wanted to go to bed, but he would never refuse his grandfather.

"I'll come," Egan volunteered. "What do you have planned for supper?"

"I got out that catfish we caught in Yaupon Creek. It's all seasoned and ready to fry. I'll go put the skillet on while you take a shower."

"Thanks," Quincy said to Egan. "I'm out for the count. See you in the morning."

Falcon and Jude went to the big house to be with their kids, and Quincy and Elias headed for bed.

"I'll help," Jericho offered.

Egan and Rico fixed supper and Grandpa gave orders with the finesse of a drill sergeant. With the old man finally asleep in his chair and the kitchen clean, Egan and Rico slipped out the back door.

Pete yapped at their feet, wanting food. Egan didn't want to give him fish, afraid he'd get a bone caught in his throat. Squatting, Egan fed him leftovers he'd found in the refrigerator—Pete's favorite.

"I'm getting some shut-eye," Rico said. "See you tomorrow."

Egan made his way to his house. The lights were out and he found his bedroom without flipping a switch. He wasn't sleepy. He was restless. And the sheets smelled like *her*. He'd meant to wash them, but hadn't had time.

His duster lay on a chair and he reached for it and his rifle. In seconds he was out the door and headed for the hills. Pete trailed behind. After a mile, the dog started to whine.

"If you're going to complain, go back to the house."

Pete barked, but kept coming.

The blackness of night was all around Egan, soothing in its own way. An owl hooted and something rustled in the bushes as crickets chirped. Familiar sounds. Calming sounds. This was his comfort zone, where no one could ever hurt him again.

He stopped when he reached the top of the hill, and spread the duster on the ground. Rachel's delicate scent reached him. It was still on the duster. She had invaded his space and Egan didn't know how to handle that. Or how to rid himself of the memories she'd left behind.

Taking a deep breath, he lay on the duster and stared at the expanse of black sky and its brilliant display of stars. Pete cozied up to him.

"I hurt her."

Pete whimpered.

"Yeah, I know. I have to talk to her before she returns to New York. I may be a lot of things, but I'm not a jerk. She deserves better from me."

Pete snuggled closer.

"Thanks, Pete. You always have the right answer." Egan scratched the dog's head and then laughed out loud at the absurdity of talking to a dog. The sound echoed through the valley and released a lot of pent-up tension. The ache in his stomach eased, too.

He pulled his hat over his face and drifted into sleep, with Rachel's sweet scent soothing him.

RACHEL HAD A nice evening with Angie. Sitting on the barstool, drinking a nonalcoholic wine cooler, she watched Angie make her special pizza. Since Angie couldn't drink, Rachel thought she wouldn't, either. They sat at the large kitchen island, eating and laughing. They talked about the past, the present and the future. Rachel didn't hold anything back and neither did Angie. They were two young girls who were now adults and had learned from their experiences.

Later, they retired to the den to watch a movie. *Love Story* just happened to be on and they both were enthralled. Every now and then Rachel's eyes would stray to Angie, who was nursing Trey. That had to be the most fulfilling experience in the world. All Rachel's hormones were kicking in and blindsiding her. Maybe it was just seeing the baby or maybe she was at the age where her biological clock was ticking overtime. But she didn't see a baby in her future anytime soon and she felt a moment of sadness.

After Trey was fed, Rachel took him from Angie and

cuddled him close. "I want one of these." She kissed Trey's cheek.

Angie stopped folding the burp cloth. "With Egan?"

"I think that ship has sailed, as they say." She tightened her arms around the sleeping baby. "There are sperm banks, you know."

Her friend gasped. "I'll pretend I didn't hear that."

"A couple of women I know in New York have chosen that route and they seem happy."

"Do you think you'll be happy without a husband?"

If he's not Egan... She cleared her throat to stop the thought. "Probably not, but that's my small-town Texas upbringing talking."

"I think it's a heartache talking."

"Yeah. I never thought I'd find the man of my dreams when I decided to come home. And I certainly never imagined that he would reject me."

"Rachel, can't you stay a little longer, until you feel better about the situation with Egan?"

"No. I've already made the plane reservation. It leaves at one on Monday." She glanced at her friend. "It's the right thing to do. I might even see a therapist when I return, to help me sort through all these conflicting feelings."

Angie didn't say anything else and they both sat there with tears in the eyes as they watched the rest of *Love Story*. Why did life have to be so sad?

ON SATURDAY, Rachel decided to give Angie and Hardy a treat. She offered to keep the kids that evening so they could have some time alone. They balked at first, but Rachel convinced them. Angie wore a black sheath dress and heels. She looked beautiful and Hardy's eyes lit up when he saw her.

After a couple hours of changing diapers, feeding and entertaining Trey, Rachel was rethinking the baby thing. But only for a second. It was pure heaven and she enjoyed every minute.

She and Erin played games, made hot-fudge sundaes and did a dance number on the Wii. It was embarrassing that Rachel couldn't keep up with a twelve-year-old. Laughing with her niece was a riot. The kids took her mind off Egan. But as soon as she went to bed that night, he was right there, with his callused hands, his gentle touch and his wounded heart.

How did she stop loving him?

THE NEXT MORNING everyone slept in, even Trey. Hardy and Erin fixed blueberry pancakes while Rachel and Angie watched. It was fun to get a glimpse of her brother interacting with his daughter. They kidded, laughed and it was clear how much they loved each other. It warmed Rachel's heart.

They were finishing breakfast when her father came into the room. He'd been in Austin and had just returned.

"You're back early," Hardy said.

The judge patted the tummy of his grandson, who was in the carrier on the kitchen island. "Rachel's leaving tomorrow and I wanted to spend some time with her."

She felt a pang of regret, but staying would help nothing. She had to get back to her life.

Her father filled a cup with coffee. "I have a phone call to make and then I'll join you."

Ever since Rachel had been home, her dad had spent a lot of time in Austin and she wondered why. Taking her plate to the sink, she asked, "What does Dad do in Austin so much?"

Hardy got up with his own plate in his hand. "I haven't had time to tell you, but Dad is seeing someone."

"Oh." Rachel looked at her brother. "That's nice. I guess she lives in Austin."

"Yeah. Dad is unaware that I know, but we're acquainted with a lot of the same people and I heard about her."

Rachel frowned. "Is it supposed to be a secret? I don't understand."

Hardy set his plate in the sink. "He hasn't actually told me he's seeing someone, so I guess he doesn't want us to know."

"That's silly. It's been twelve years. I'm not upset that he's dating anyone. Are you?"

"No." Hardy leaned against the counter. "I've never brought up the subject. I thought if he wanted to talk about it, he would. It's his life and I didn't want to intrude on his privacy."

"Is it someone we know?"

"You remember Judge Janson?"

"Yeah." Rachel picked up her cup of coffee.

"He died about five years ago and Dad is seeing his widow. They've been seen around Austin. That's all I know."

A chill ran through Rachel and the cup she was holding hit the floor and shattered across the tiles. Hardy jumped back and Angie ran to get a broom and a dustpan."

Not Liz Janson. It couldn't be. Hardy and Angie worked to clean up the mess, but Rachel was caught in a web of the past.

"You okay, Aunt Rachel?" Erin asked.

She heard her niece's voice, but all she could see was her mother's face. Angie came to the rescue. "Erin, take the baby upstairs and put him in his bed. He's already asleep, but stay with him awhile."

"Okay, Mama."

As Erin left the room with Trey, Angie guided Rachel to a chair. "What's wrong?"

Rachel looked at Hardy. "Dad is seeing Liz Janson."

"Yes. Why is it making you so upset? You said you didn't care."

"How long do you think he's been seeing her?"

Hardy shrugged. "I don't know. A few years, maybe."

"And all this time he hasn't mentioned her to you?"

"No. What are you getting at?"

Rachel jumped to her feet. "I need to talk to Dad." She ran out of the kitchen.

"Rachel," Hardy called from a few steps behind her.

In the study, their dad was on his cell phone, a lit cigar in an ashtray. The pungent smell reached Rachel—a well-remembered scent from when she was a child. It reminded her of her father, his big bear hugs and that secure feeling she got whenever he held her. But today all she felt was an anger she couldn't control. And she saw no need to attempt to do so.

"Rachel." Her father was startled and clicked off the phone.

"How long have you been seeing Liz Janson?"

His eyebrows knotted together. "Sweetheart, what's this about?"

"Rachel, leave this alone," Hardy said from behind her.

"I will, just as soon as I hear Dad's answer."

"What does it matter?" the judge asked.

"It matters a great deal," Rachel told him. "Please answer the question. And I expect complete honesty, just as you have preached for years to us and to everyone who ever came into your courtroom."

The judge got to his feet, his robust features pale. "My private life is my own business and I don't bring it into my home around my children."

Anger bubbled up inside Rachel and she couldn't hold her tongue. She pointed at her father. "You've been seeing Liz Janson for more than twelve years. You cheated on our mother and she *knew*."

"What?" The paleness on her father's face turned a deadly white.

Hardy took her arm. "That's enough, Rachel."

She jerked her arm away. "What are you afraid of, Hardy? The truth?" She glanced at her father. "Tell us the truth. You demanded it in your courtroom, so why not in your home?"

The judge glanced down at the cigar burning in the ashtray. "You obviously know something I don't."

"Yes. About two months before Mom died I came home from school early and found her crying in her bedroom. She said she didn't feel well, but I knew something was up with her. We talked and she finally admitted that she thought you were seeing someone else. That she felt old and ugly because you liked younger women with big breasts, like Liz Janson."

"No-o-o." A denial came from her father.

"Yes. She told me you were always joking and laughing with her when you had those many dinners with the elderly judge and his wife. Then Mom found lipstick on your suit jacket and it wasn't hers. It was Liz's. She remembered the color. I told her she was being silly and for her to ask you. But she didn't, did she?"

The judge sank into his chair, at a loss for words perhaps for the first time in his life.

"Dad, is this true?" Hardy asked, looking as pale as his father. The truth was sometimes hard to bear.

The judge cleared his throat. "It…it just happened."

"Oh, please, isn't that a standard reply from all men? I expected better from you," Rachel declared.

"Sweetheart, please listen to me. I loved your mother and—"

Rachel shook her head. "No, that line's not going to work, either."

"You cheated on our mother." Hardy came out of his stupor, shaking his head. "She was the most loving, caring person in the world. She campaigned tirelessly for you for years. She spearheaded so many fund-raisers and spent days on the road encouraging people to vote for a man of honor, a man of integrity, a family man. Ha, what a crock that was. I can't believe you could do this to her."

"Son, I…" The judge buried his face in his hands. "I'm guilty as charged. Your mother and I had grown apart in those last years." With his mouth covered, his voice was muffled, but Rachel and Hardy understood every word. "She had her interests and I had mine."

"Yes." Rachel snickered. "Yours was Liz and Mom's was helping other people, mainly you. If your marriage had grown stale, you should have done something to spice it up, like a weekend away or a trip somewhere together, instead of always thinking about your career."

She drew a hot breath. "For years I blamed myself for Mother's death, but it wasn't my fault. When she was walking out of that mall with the sexiest dress she could find to outshine Liz, she wasn't thinking about anything but making you notice her again. That's why her perception was off. That's why she walked right into a fight between gang members. Other people were running for cover, but she was distracted. I will never forgive you for that."

Rachel tore from the room and headed for the garage.

She didn't know where she was going, but she had to get away to deal with all the anger inside her. And she didn't even know if that was possible.

ON SUNDAYS, any Rebel sons on the ranch were required to have lunch with their mother. She always cooked a big meal, enough for everyone. There was no way to get out of it if they wanted peace in the family. Egan placed his hat on his head and headed for the big house.

His mom had prime rib steaks going on the grill in the kitchen, and the smell was mouthwatering. The family gathered in the dining room at the big table that seated fourteen. His mother sat at the head of the table and Falcon sat at the other end, with Eden on his right and Grandpa on his left. The others took their seats on the sides, along with Jericho. He was always welcome. Egan sat between Quincy and Jude. Zane was next to his dad.

"It's nice to have most of my boys for lunch," Kate said. "Paxton and Phoenix should be home today."

"We could use their help." Falcon cut into his steak. "I talked to Sanchez and he and his boys will be here tomorrow morning to start cutting the coastal in the west pasture. It's going to take all of us to get the hay in for winter. We'll be baling into June and maybe July."

"Everyone will pull their weight, son," their mother told him.

"They better." Elias stuffed steak into his mouth. "Paxton and Phoenix need to slack off on rodeoing for a while."

"They do very well," Kate said. "But we will need their help." She passed a dish of potatoes to Quincy. "We still have to watch our finances. The note is coming due on the Fitzwater place. Buying it was a good deal, since it's across the road from our property, but sometimes it's a strain to come up with that money. I was thinking we might tear that old house down. The lumber might be worth something."

Egan jerked up his head. "Why? I like the house. It was built around 1870 and some of the lumber in it is very good."

"Are you going to fix it up?" Falcon asked.

"I might." Egan gripped his tea glass. "It might be a nice place for me to live. I'd like my own home one day."

Silence followed his words and he glanced at the startled faces of the others. "What? Try living with Elias and you'll know what I'm talking about."

"Hey. I resent that." But Elias was smiling. "Can I rent your room out to someone then?"

"Hell, no," Quincy quickly replied. "And stop stretching out your long legs. You're scratching my boots."

"Like I care."

"If I put a fist in your face, you'll care."

"Stop it," their mother said. "I won't have any fighting on a Sunday."

"Yes, ma'am." Elias sat up straight.

Kate turned her attention to Egan. "If you want to fix the house up on your own time, then do so, and I hope your brothers might help you."

"Ah, man." Elias was not pleased.

"I will do it a little bit at a time," Egan said. "And no help is required."

His mother gave him a sharp glance, but didn't say anything more and the meal continued.

"Did I tell y'all about the time—"

"Abe, please, no stories at the dinner table," Kate interrupted.

"Bossy damn woman," Grandpa muttered under his breath.

"Dad, after lunch can I go into town to see my friends?" Eden asked. At seventeen, she was eager for freedom.

"No." Falcon took a sip of tea.

"Dad!"

He gave his daughter his full attention. "I let you go last week and what did you do?"

Eden looked down at her plate. "It wasn't my fault."

"I trusted you to be home by six and you weren't. I had to call. You broke the rules so you pay. It won't hurt you to spend Sunday with your family."

"She just wants to see Brandon Lee." Zane rolled his eyes, clearly enjoying teasing his cousin. "He's so handsome."

Eden pointed a finger at Zane. "You're dead meat." She jumped out of her chair and ran toward him, but Zane was a step ahead of her. Round and round the table they ran until Jude reached out, caught the back of his son's shirt and pulled him into his chair.

"I don't like you tattling on your cousin."

"Aw, Dad."

"Zane's a jerk." Eden plopped into her chair.

"Who's Brandon Lee?" Falcon asked.

"Nobody," she mumbled.

"And he's going to stay that way."

"When I turn eighteen, I'm leaving and never coming—"

Everyone at the table saw the ghost tiptoe across Falcon's face, even his daughter. Eden threw herself at him, wrapping her arms around his neck. "I didn't mean it, Daddy. I'll never leave you like she did. Never."

Falcon patted her back. "I know, baby."

The rattle of a trailer interrupted the moment. Paxton and Phoenix were home. It didn't take long before they were charging into the dining room with plates in their hands.

"You better take care of those horses in the trailer," Grandpa warned.

"Don't you have any respect for your mother?" Falcon asked. "You could have called and let her know you were coming home so early."

"Give it a rest, Falcon." Paxton slid into a chair.

Phoenix sat across from him. "I'm not roping anymore with Pax. All he does is chat up girls, and we don't place in the money. He's not focused. Rope with me, Egan. You're better than he is any way."

Egan dropped his napkin on the table and got to his feet. "No, thanks, lil' brother, my rodeo days are over." He went to his mother, leaned over and kissed her cheek. "Thanks for lunch, Mom." He walked out of the dining room, but their voices followed.

"Does anyone remember the last time Egan smiled?" Elias asked.

"When he kicked your ass the other day in the barn," Paxton replied.

"Shut up."

"When did this happen?" their mother asked.

Egan closed the door and welcomed the resulting quiet. Pete jumped around at his feet.

Jericho caught up with him. "Where you going?"

"Thought I'd ride over and check out the Fitzwater place. I haven't been there in a while."

"You serious about fixing it up?"

"Yeah. It gets a little crowded around here. That's why we're always fighting."

They walked side by side to the barn. "It's better to fight than to keep all that angst locked up inside."

Egan opened the corral gate and whistled for Gypsy. "Well, then, the Rebels will never need a therapist."

Rico laughed, something he rarely did. "I'm gonna take a nap and then round up those heifers that need to go to La Grange in the morning. That will give us a head start."

Egan guided Gypsy into a stall. "After I look at the house, I'll help you. It won't take long."

Rico eyed him.

"What?"

"Nothing." His friend shrugged. "Just trying to figure out why you're interested in the house all of a sudden, but it's none of my business. I'm glad to have a roof over my head. Glad to have a family. That's my sermon for the day. See you later."

Egan threw a blanket over Gypsy and then a saddle. His interest in the house had nothing to do with Rachel. That's what Jericho wanted him to say. There was nothing wrong with wanting his own place.

Shooting out from the barn with Pete behind him, Egan knew he had to see Rachel today. He didn't know when she was leaving, but he had to make his peace with her. They'd bonded in an unusual kind of way and he didn't want her to have bad feelings about him.

Then he would put her out of his mind.

Chapter Fourteen

Rachel's tears blinded her and she couldn't see the road. Wiping them away, she tried to figure out where she was. Then she saw the sign: Rebel Road. She was going to Egan. And he didn't want to see her. A choked sob left her throat as she searched for a place to turn around.

Her world didn't have an anchor anymore. Home had provided a security that had kept her going, had kept her grounded. And home was all a lie. Her parents didn't have the perfect marriage, as she'd believed, as they had portrayed to the world. A fallacy her parents had built over the years.

At the moment, her whole life seemed like a lie. And she had to wonder if there had been other women for her father. Why did people even bother to get married? She wanted a marriage that would last forever. One where the fire would never die and one where the love was everlasting. Was there such a thing? Or was she just naive?

She had to come to grips with all this, but right now she felt adrift in the sea of lies and deception, and didn't know if she could ever forgive her father.

The wooded areas on both sides of the road were owned by the Rebels. Rachel didn't see a cattle guard or entrance where she could turn around. She was thinking of using the ditch when she noticed a truck behind her, a beat-up old one with a rusty right fender. She slowed down so the driver could pass, but when the vehicle came alongside her it bumped into her car and forced her into the ditch. She slammed on the brakes and the car came to a sudden stop. Before she could gather her wits, the door was yanked open and a man grabbed her arm, pulling her out.

Panic gripped her and she fought back, trying to get free. She slapped with her hands and kicked with her feet until he got a choke hold around her neck. Her throat burned and she couldn't breath.

Something cold was placed against her temple. A gun! Oh, no! What did he want? He smelled of liquor and garlic, and her stomach churned with nausea.

"Be still, missy, and nothin' will happen to ya."

"Who are you? What do you want?"

"Isadore McCray, and now yer gonna tell the sheriff the truth. I'm not going to jail."

The crazy man with the dogs. Fury slowly built in her and she again tried to twist out of his grasp. He tightened his hold and she coughed, struggling to breathe.

"Stop or I'll break yer neck."

Rachel tried to think rationally, but her heart was racing so fast her brain could barely function. He wanted her to go to the sheriff with him; that much she could grasp. She just had to reason with him and everything would be okay. But she knew she had to be careful or the crazy man could really hurt her.

EGAN RODE TOWARD the Fitzwater property. He pulled up when he heard Pete yapping. The dog was about fifty yards behind him and had run out of energy.

Egan patted his leg. "Come on, boy. You can do it."

Pete loped toward him. When he reached Egan, he

looked up and whined. Egan patted his leg again and Pete jumped into the air, not quite making it high enough.

"Come on, boy," Egan repeated. This time he reached down, caught a front paw and pulled him onto the saddle. The dog's heart beat wildly against his hand.

"I'm going to have to stop feeding you so much. It's making you lazy."

Pete whimpered and rested his muzzle close to the saddle horn, looking straight ahead. Gypsy raised her head, getting antsy. Egan kneed her and they were off. Something through the woods near the fence line caught his attention. It was white and looked like a car. He turned Gypsy in that direction.

As he drew closer, he recognized the Mustang. It was Rachel's. Had she run off into the ditch? When he sensed something wasn't right, he stopped, dismounted and removed his rifle from the scabbard.

"Stay here," he said to Pete, and made his way on foot. He squatted in the grass and surveyed the scene. Izzy had Rachel! The crazy fool. What was he up to? McCray had an arm around her neck and a gun pointed at her head. Oh, man.

Egan pulled his phone out of his pocket and called Wyatt. Luckily, the sheriff answered.

"You better get out to Rebel Road. Izzy has Rachel and he has a gun. I'm going in." Egan clicked off before Wyatt could tell him otherwise. No way was he letting Rachel get hurt.

He had a problem, though. How was he going to get Izzy's attention without the fool shooting Rachel or him? He needed a distraction. He motioned to Pete and the dog trotted over. Now he would find out if Pete really could understand him.

Rubbing the dog's head, he said, "Listen close, boy.

This is important." He pointed to a post in the fence. "I want you to go there and bark. Do you understand me? Go to the fence post and bark and then go back to Gypsy."

Pete whimpered and rubbed his face against Egan's jeans.

"Go to the post. Wait for my signal and bark. Go!"

Pete whimpered again and showed no signs of obeying.

"Go. Wait. Bark. Now!"

Pete turned around in a circle and then made a dash for the fence post, except he went to the wrong one. It was farther down, but that didn't matter. It was far enough away. Egan moved toward the fence. As he reached it, he held up his hand, giving Pete the signal.

Like magic, the dog barked and barked. Damn, the dog *could* understand him.

"What's that?" Izzy turned toward the sound.

Wasting no time, Egan leaped over the fence and stood in the middle of the blacktop road with the rifle in his hand. He didn't aim it at Izzy, afraid he'd shoot Rachel if he did so. Instead he held it by his side, the barrel pointed toward the ground. But his forefinger was on the trigger.

"Let her go, Izzy."

The man swung toward him. "Rebel, what are ya doing here?"

"Let her go."

He tightened his arm around Rachel's neck and she coughed. "She's coming with me. She's gonna tell the sheriff the truth."

"About what?"

"I didn't sic my dogs on her. She lied."

Egan had to be careful what he said. The guy didn't have both oars in the water.

"Why did the dogs attack her, then?"

"It was an accident."

"Accident?"

"I said 'pretty fresh meat' under my breath and I didn't think they could hear me, but they did and I couldn't stop 'em. It was an accident."

"Pretty fresh meat? That's what you say to your dogs when you're trespassing on Rebel land and see a newborn calf that is defenseless."

"Your family deserves it," Izzy shouted, and the gun shook against Rachel's temple.

Egan held back his anger for her sake. "I'm sure Ms. Hollister would be willing to talk to the sheriff without you using force. That just kind of muddies the water, if you know what I mean."

"Go away or I'll shoot her."

The old man was close to losing it. That meant anything could happen and that was dangerous.

The blare of a siren split the air and Izzy backed up to his truck, still holding on to Rachel. Egan had to calm him down.

"That's the sheriff, Izzy. Ms. Hollister can talk to him now, so you can put the gun down. She's willing to do that, I'm sure."

"Y-yes," she spluttered.

The sheriff's car whizzed to a stop not far from Izzy's truck. It was followed by Ira and Gunnar McCray, and then Falcon, Quincy and Jericho. They had a full house. News spread fast. Wyatt got out of his cruiser, as did Stuart. The sheriff didn't carry a gun, so Egan thought he must feel positive he could talk to Izzy.

"Put the rifle down, Egan," Wyatt said.

Egan was taken aback for a moment. "I'll put my gun down when Izzy does, and not before."

"He's causing trouble, Sheriff," Izzy told him.

"What are you doing, Izzy?" Ira joined the conversation. "Let that girl go. You're only making this worse."

"She has to talk to the sheriff, Ira. I can't go to jail."

Wyatt walked closer. "I'm here, Izzy. Now put the gun down."

Instead, Izzy pressed it into Rachel's temple, and from where Egan was standing he could see her trembling. His gut tightened. "Tell him I had nothing to do with the dogs attacking ya."

"I…I…"

"Loosen your hold. You're choking her to death." Wyatt moved a little closer. "Are you okay, Rachel?"

She didn't respond and Egan wanted to raise his rifle and rain holy hell on the McCrays. But he remained still, waiting for a moment when the gun was pointed away from Rachel.

"It's him who should be in jail." Izzy nodded toward Egan. "He took her from the car and killed my dogs."

"He didn't take me," Rachel gasped. "My car broke down and he helped me."

"Shut up." Izzy tightened his hold and her face turned red.

"Them was good dogs. He should die."

Almost in slow motion Egan saw the gun leave Rachel's temple and move toward him. In a split second he raised his rifle and fired, knocking the weapon from Izzy's hand. But not before Izzy's gun fired, knocking Egan backward onto the blacktop. His ears rang and his heart pounded as shouts echoed around him.

Rachel screamed and Wyatt and Stuart jumped Izzy and had him on the ground in a second. Stuart handcuffed the man and jerked him to his feet.

"It's him. He should be in jail," Izzy kept mumbling,

as Ira and Gunnar ran to his side. "Ira, don't let 'em put me in jail."

"Sheriff…" Ira turned to Wyatt in appeal and that's when Egan lost consciousness.

When he came to, Rachel, Wyatt, Falcon, Quincy and Jericho were staring down at him. He blinked and Rachel bent and hugged him. "Are you okay?"

He wasn't sure. He didn't feel pain anywhere, so he must have not been shot. Falcon and Jericho helped him to his feet and Quincy showed him his hat. A bullet hole went through it.

"Damn, that's my good hat."

"Better your hat than you," Wyatt said, and shook his head. "That was some fine shooting. You hit the gun and knocked it right out of his hand."

"The Rebels know how to use a gun," Gunnar said. "They're good at killing people."

That lit Falcon's fuse. "We wouldn't have to if some people wouldn't try to kill innocent children."

"Go home, Gunnar." Wyatt got between them. "The skirmish between the Rebels and McCrays is over for the day."

Gunnar went back to his father, who was talking to Izzy in the backseat of the squad car.

Wyatt reached for his phone. "I'm calling for an ambulance. I'd feel better if both of you were seen by a doctor."

"No, thanks," Egan said. "I'm fine."

"I am, too," Rachel added.

Wyatt slipped his phone back into its case. "You have a right to refuse, but you have to come in and give a statement of what happened here today."

"I'll tell you what happened here today." Rachel's voice was high, indicating she was angry. "That crazy man sicced his dogs on me and then he wanted me to lie about it so he wouldn't have to go to jail. He must've followed me from my house, so that means he's been watching me for some time." She ran her hands up her arms. "That scares the hell out of me! And then you have the nerve to tell Egan to put his gun down. What did you think was going to happen then, Wyatt?"

"I was trying to defuse the situation. Less guns. Less trouble," he told her.

"You know, the more time I spend in this one-horse town, the more I realize that justice is blind, deaf and ignorant, and I just—"

Egan touched her arm. "Relax. Wyatt was just doing his job."

She ran both hands through her blond hair and everyone could see she was shaken. "I…"

"Maybe it's best if you see a doctor," Egan suggested. Her eyes flashed at him, but only for a moment. Hardy and her dad drove up, and her attention was diverted. Her brother ran to them.

"Rachel, are you okay?"

She took a deep breath. "Yes."

"What's going on here, Wyatt?" the judge asked.

Instead of answering, he said, "I'm taking Izzy in. Feel free to explain to your father. I'm done here."

In a calm and steady voice Rachel told her dad what had happened, but Egan noted she was still extremely upset.

"Sweetheart, come home. You need to see a doctor."

Rachel bristled even more. "I'm only going to say this one more time. I'm fine."

"Then let's go home. We'll get your car later."

"I'll come home when I'm ready."

A lot of tension was flying back and forth and Egan

knew something had happened in the Hollister family for Rachel to be this upset.

"Rachel…" Hardy made an attempt to talk to her, to no avail.

"After I talk to Egan, I'll be home."

Hardy and the judge exchange glances and then walked to their truck, which surprised Egan. Why weren't they trying to take care of Rachel?

"We'll see y'all later," Falcon said, and walked toward his vehicle, followed by Quincy. Jericho hung behind.

Egan gave him a dark stare and his friend got the message, heading off after Egan's brothers. That left him and Rachel standing in the middle of the blacktop road.

She took another deep breath. "Could we talk for a minute? And for the record, I'm not falling apart. I'm just angry."

"I think everyone knows that. Is there a reason besides Izzy kidnapping you?"

RACHEL WASN'T SURE how to answer that, or if she should at all. She walked over to the Mustang, which was half in the ditch, and sat on the grass beside it. Egan picked up his rifle and sank down next to her. She wrestled with her conscience and in the end knew she had to tell someone. And that Egan would understand in his own easygoing way.

"A lot has happened since I saw you last," she said, trying to wipe a stain from her white pants.

"I gathered that."

She told him about her father and his mistress, and anger filled every word. She couldn't hold it back.

Egan drew up his knees and studied the blacktop in front of him. "I'm sorry," he finally said. "It has to be rough on you. I've only known you a little while and I know how much you loved your mother."

"My mother knew and that's what hurts the most. She had to have been miserable, knowing my father didn't desire her anymore. And that there was a younger woman he was interested in, one she had to meet on a regular basis. Men are pigs."

Egan looked at her then, his dark eyes gleaming. "Women say that a lot."

"Because it's true. I want a forever kind of love. Is that foolish and unrealistic?"

"I don't know anything about love. Few men do, is my opinion. We get the physical side, but all the emotion eludes us." His eyes held hers. "I'm sorry I hurt you. I handled our relationship badly and I regret that."

"At least you're honest…up to a point."

"What do you mean?"

"You deny yourself a life because you're afraid. Life hasn't been all that kind to you, but one day you'll have to step back into the real world and stop hiding out on Rebel Ranch."

He didn't answer and she knew that he wouldn't. He just kept staring at the blacktop. It was a warm May day and she welcomed the breeze that cooled her heated emotions.

She decided to drop the personal stuff about him because it was getting them nowhere. Nowhere was where they would always be. "After the argument with my father, I just drove off, needing to get away. I had no idea where I was until I looked up and saw Rebel Road. I was coming to you, because I knew you would understand. I did that without thinking, and that's a little jarring since, as you say, we barely know each other."

"Rachel—"

"I know we can never be together, so you don't have to explain that again. My father hurt you. He has hurt a lot of people, but I have to believe that, in his own way, he thought he was doing the right thing that day he sent you to prison."

"What?"

"I'm not saying it was right. I'm saying it was right for him. And I'm not defending my father. He thought in his own mind he was deterring you from a life of crime, keeping you away from the crowd who had led you astray. He's seen a lot of that in his courtroom. I don't think it had anything to do with your father."

Egan moved restlessly and she knew she'd stirred up something he'd never thought of before.

"I'm not saying that to hurt you."

"I know you're not."

Silence ebbed away into a place they both knew would happen: the final goodbye.

"My plane leaves tomorrow at one, so I guess this will be the last time I'll see you. I've thanked you several times, but I'm not sure if you understand how much it's meant to me, getting to know you."

Again, he didn't say anything.

"Thank you for today, too. I don't know what would've happened if you hadn't come along. You've risked your life twice for me and 'thank you' doesn't seem enough."

"It is," he said, staring at his hands, locked over his knees. "This is going to sound odd, but I hope you can forgive your father before you leave. Carrying around all that anger is not good. It's best to let it go."

She glanced at him. "Then why can't you?"

"My situation is different. I was hurt physically by your father's insensitivity."

Silence stretched again as they both dealt with their

own thoughts. A blackbird landed on the fence and they both watched it as they came to grips with parting. Or at least Rachel did. She was never sure about Egan. She could never pinpoint what he was feeling.

There was nothing left to say, so Rachel got to her feet. He stood tall and strong, and she could almost feel those invisible walls he'd built around himself. He wasn't letting her in. He wasn't letting anyone in. Her heart sank at the thought and she finally had to admit there was no future with Egan.

Unable to resist, she moved into his arms and wrapped hers around his waist, resting her face against his chest. "I'll never forget you."

It surprised her when his arms went around her and he gripped her tightly. "I hope you find the life you deserve."

The manly scent of sweat and soap stirred her senses and she reached up and kissed him. He kissed her back and they stood there holding each other, lips on lips, heart on heart, saying goodbye in a way they both understood.

She drew back and gazed into his passion-filled eyes. Why couldn't he admit what he was feeling? And then she knew. She took a step backward. "If you think about it, Egan, you'll see that my father is not the one standing between us. It's you. You won't allow yourself to love. You won't allow yourself a life. That's so sad." She touched his lips with her forefinger. "Goodbye, Egan." Tears clogged her voice and she walked to the Mustang and got in.

The car backed out of the ditch easily. She didn't look at Egan as she passed him. There was no need. There was no point looking back. She had to go forward and face a future without him. She just had to be strong enough to do it—alone.

Chapter Fifteen

Rachel went home, because she didn't want her family to worry about her. Being kidnapped had given her a new perspective on life. Her parents had portrayed a good marriage for their kids. They'd wanted them to grow up feeling loved and wanted. And they'd succeeded. She still had to sort out her issues with her father.

Three pairs of worried eyes met her as she came through the back door. She hugged Angie and said, "I just need some time alone, please. Make everyone understand that." Then she went upstairs to her room. Even though Angie was quiet and sweet, she had an inner strength that didn't bode well for anyone who tried to cross her.

Rachel lay on her bed and thought about the future. Egan had said that maybe she needed to feel the guilt so she could deal with her mother's death. That was probably true. Her mother's life had centered around Rachel. In the summertime, they'd gone on vacations together. Her father was always busy and she and her mother had enjoyed shopping and visiting other countries.

Looking back with twenty-twenty vision, she realized all the signs of a marriage on the rocks had been there. Her parents never really spent any time together except at political fund-raisers and events that had to do with her

father's career. At other times her mother was busy working with charities and catering to Rachel's every whim.

What a spoiled brat she'd been. Rachel got up and
looked out the window at the beautiful swimming pool
in the landscaped yard, all designed by her mother. She
had put so much of herself in everything she'd done.
Why couldn't she have put that effort into her marriage?

Rachel ran her hands over her face as she realized her
confused thoughts were shifting and her issue with her
father was changing. Nothing gave a man the right to
break his marriage vows. What would've happened if her
parents had divorced? The family would've been thrown
into chaos and Rachel's life wouldn't have been so idyllic. And that had been her mother's main goal. How Rachel wished there had been some compromise along the
way, and that her mother had been as interested in her
marriage as she'd been in raising her children.

She and Rachel had been friends more than mother
and daughter. They'd laughed, shared secrets and had
good times together. What wasn't idyllic about that?
Maybe being told no once in a while would've benefited
Rachel more than anything.

What was she doing? She ran her fingers through her
hair, the conflicting thoughts torturing her.

Walking around the room, she tried to dredge up all
that anger toward her father that she had felt earlier. It
wasn't there anymore. Maybe she was just tired of feeling guilty. Feeling angry. Everybody made mistakes and
her father had made a big one. But she wasn't going to
judge him any longer. That wasn't her place. She would
return to New York and build her own life. That's all that
was left for her now.

She picked up the drawing of Egan on her desk. "One
day you will be a memory. A beautiful memory I can

tell my children about. The handsome, brave cowboy who saved my life." She touched the picture. "Goodbye, Egan."

At dusk, a knock sounded at the door and Hardy entered with a tray of food. "I'm not staying, but Angie insisted you have something to eat."

"It's okay." She motioned for him to step into the room. "I'm better now. I just needed to do some thinking."

He set the tray on her desk. "I'm having a hard time dealing with all this, too. I had a talk with Dad and learned some things I never knew before."

Rachel sat on the bed. "Like what?"

He pulled out the desk chair and took a seat. "The fact that he cheated on our mother has hit me hard. I always thought Dad was a one-woman man—like me."

"And you're worried you might cheat on Angie one day?"

He frowned. "I would never do that, but I wanted answers. Did you know that Dad and Mom had an arranged marriage?"

"What?"

"Dad was thirty-two and a bachelor when his father said it was time for him to get married, and that he'd picked out the woman. She was educated, polished and her family had connections—just the type of woman he needed to further his political career."

Rachel was aghast. She'd never dreamed such a thing.

"Dad said they grew to love each other over the years and it was a good marriage in a lot of ways. They had us and Dad had the political career he wanted."

"I don't think we ever really knew our parents, Hardy."

Her brother rubbed his hands together. "It feels that way. Dad could see that I was concerned about my own marriage. I love Angie with all my heart and I just can't see myself ever doing that to her."

"And?"

"Dad said I didn't have to worry about following in his footsteps in that area. That I'd married the woman of my heart. And he's right about that. I waited ten years for Angie and I would never do anything to see that look in her eyes that you had yesterday—a look of total devastation."

Rachel got up and sat on her brother's lap. "And I would have to kill you."

They laughed together and it was a release of all the tension of the day. They were going to make it.

"I wish you weren't going," Hardy said.

"I have to get back to my life."

He touched the blue marks on her throat. "Are you sure you're okay?"

"Yeah," she said, with more enthusiasm than she was feeling. It would be a long time before she would be okay again.

If ever…

THE NEXT MORNING Rachel got up early and packed. Then she went into town to talk to Wyatt. She had to apologize for her rude outburst yesterday. He was very understanding, as always. She gave a statement and Wyatt took photos of her bruised neck and said he would be in touch with details about the trial, if there was one. But his feeling was that Izzy would be put into a mental institution.

With her suitcases in the kitchen, she had one more thing to do. Taking a deep breath, she walked into the study, where her father was drinking Scotch.

He looked up, his eyes tired and bloodshot. Her heart took a hit at the sight.

"Hardy's driving me to the airport," she said. "I can't leave without saying goodbye."

"I appreciate that."

"I said I would never forgive you, but that was in the heat of the moment. I had your marriage on a pedestal as an example for the world, but it was far from that. I can see that now. I suppose you both did the best you could. And I guess I understand better since Hardy told me the truth."

The judge's brows knotted. "What did Hardy say?"

"That you had an arranged marriage."

"It was much more, sweetheart. I want you to know that."

"I do and…and I forgive you. I had no right to judge you. You and Mom gave me a good childhood. Now I have to live my own life." She reached into her purse, pulled out a credit card and placed it in front of him. "I won't need this anymore, and please stop paying my rent in New York. If I'm going to be independent, I have to make it on my own."

"Sweetheart, there's no need."

She shook her head. "There's every need. You see, I'm supposed to be an adult now, so it's time to cut the apron strings and the financial ones, also."

He pushed the card toward her. "I'd feel better if you kept it."

Ignoring the card, she walked around the desk and hugged him. He held her in a fierce grip and it took a moment before he would let go.

"Goodbye, Dad. I'll call when I can."

She walked out with her heart in shreds, but she felt better about herself than she had in a very long time.

AFTER A LONG day of building fences, Egan was dog tired again, and he liked it that way. He couldn't think. But every now and then Rachel's words slipped through the tiredness.

My father is not the one standing between us. It's you.

He thought in his own mind he was deterring you from a life of crime, keeping you away from the crowd who had led you astray.

"You okay?" Rico asked, and Egan realized he'd been staring off into space.

He leaned on the horse stall, knowing he had to talk to someone and Rico was the logical person. He wouldn't judge him. "Can I ask you a question?"

Rico hung a bridle on the barn wall. "Sure."

Egan pushed back his hat slightly. He hated his new hat. He'd had it for days and he still hadn't broken it in, so it wasn't comfortable. His old one had been a part of him.

"Don't answer right away. Think about it for a minute."

"Okay." Rico stood on the other side of the stall, watching him.

"Do you think Judge Hollister was right in sentencing me to prison? No." He held up his hand. "What I mean is do you think the judge thought he was fair in my sentencing, and it had nothing to do with my father?"

Rico placed his forearms on the stall and leaned in slightly, as if deep in thought. "I'm thinking, like you asked. I'm going to be honest, because I know you want me to. When I first met you in prison, you had an attitude. That's what prompted you getting your head pushed into a toilet. Big Joe didn't like any lip from a kid."

"I guess I had a chip on my shoulder."

"A big one and it almost got you killed. You were fighting mad at what had been done to you and your life, and you took it out on everyone, even men twice your size and three times as mean."

"If I was that bad, why did you champion me?" Egan had never had the chance to ask that question of his friend, and he desperately wanted an answer.

"If anyone needed a champion, you did, and I don't like bullies. Besides, I saw a lot of me as a teenager in you. Striking back when I couldn't do anything else. But once I got to know you, the inner you who was struggling with your father's death, we formed a connection that will never be broken."

Egan nodded, not upset with his friend, because he knew he spoke the truth.

"And if I remember correctly, you told me the crowd you were running with in college was pretty rough. They were into drugs and illegal activities, but you had resisted so far. How long do you think that would've lasted?"

It was like looking at the past through a mirror. Egan had been young, and angry that his father had died, and he'd been lashing out at everyone. He would start drinking in the mornings and when he fell into bed at night he'd be stone drunk. That was the only way to forget that his father was gone.

"You were already smoking marijuana every now and then, and believe me, I know what drugs can do. I've been there and lived through it all. You know that. Anything I'm saying is only to help you."

"I know, man. I've had this hatred and resentment in me for so many years, and I'm beginning to wonder who I've been more angry with—myself or Judge Hollister."

"Only you can answer that. But if you want answers, you have to talk to the man himself."

"Thanks, Jericho. I…"

"I know, man, you don't have to explain anything to me. I'm always here if you need anything."

He inclined his head and Jericho walked out of the

barn. So many thoughts warred inside Egan, but his friend was right. It was time to face Judge Hollister and let all the resentment go, just as he'd told Rachel.

She'd been gone almost a week now and a day didn't go by that he didn't think about her. He wondered how long it would be before that stopped. It had to soon or the memories would drive him crazy. Maybe if he washed the sheets on his bed it would help. Somehow, he kept putting it off, spending time in the woods without a bed, thinking that the memories would fade. So far, he wasn't having any luck.

Pete whined at his feet and Egan bent down to rub the dog's head. "What do you think, boy? Is it time to face my past?"

Pete barked.

"Yeah, I thought so."

On Sunday morning he drove over to the Hollisters', one place he said he would never go, but he had to face the man. Since it was Sunday, he was hoping to catch the judge alone. It was well known that Hardy and Angie attended church regularly.

Egan rang the doorbell of the big two-story home. No one answered, so he rang it a couple more times. He was about to go back to his truck when the door swung open.

"What...oh, Mr. Rebel." The judge stood there in his pajamas and bathrobe, with a glass of liquor in his hand. His gray hair was tousled and his features were drawn and haggard. He didn't even resemble the judge that Egan remembered.

"Could I speak to you for a minute?" he asked, wondering if he'd made a big mistake in coming here. The man didn't look to be in a talkative mood.

The judge held up his glass. "Come on in. I'll pour you a drink."

Egan followed him through a large foyer and then into a study. The man reached for a glass in the liquor cabinet.

Egan held up his hand. "No, thanks."

The judge downed the rest of the liquor in his glass and poured himself another round. "What's on your mind? Is it about Rachel?"

"No. I'd like to talk about something else."

He sank into his chair. "Go ahead. I have all the time in the world."

"I'd like to talk about the sentence you gave me all those years ago."

"It was overturned, so I don't see why you have questions."

"At the time I thought the sentence was severe and that you were being judgmental because of my father. You actually mentioned violence in my family, so what else was I to think?"

The judge leaned forward, a keen look in his eyes. "That remark was out of line and that's the reason the case was thrown out. I crossed a line for the first time in my career."

"Why did you do that?"

He shrugged and studied the liquor in his glass. "I was having one of those bad days that most judges have. I'd had another case about six months previous. A young man had beaten his wife severely. She forgave him and asked for leniency. Instead of jail time, I ordered a year of counseling. They were going to work on their marriage. That morning I'd heard that he'd beaten her to death."

Egan was speechless. He always heard there were two sides to every story, but this was hitting him where he lived—in his heart.

The judge took a drink from the glass. "I went over your records thoroughly. You were into a lot of trouble in college, DUIs, drinking, fighting, smoking drugs and sneaking into girls' dorms, causing trouble. Your friends' records were even worse. You said you didn't know the guys who robbed the liquor store and killed the man. But they were at that party just like you, and you all mingled with the same crowd of troublemakers. You were headed down a one-way street. Warning lights were flashing, but you didn't see any of them. You were indignant that anyone would accuse you of anything."

Egan sank into a leather chair behind him. The mirror now had a spotlight and he could see the past so clearly. He'd built himself up in his mind as the victim, when in fact he'd been part of the problem. Oh, man.

"Do you remember that day I sentenced you?"

"Of course. It's branded on my brain. You said I needed to be taught a lesson."

"I said you needed to learn responsibility for your actions, and prison would give you time to think about what was happening in your life. I knew you'd spend a few months there before your family would get you out. Time enough for you to think about your future and what had happened. Do you remember what occurred next?"

Egan stared down at his callused hands. "Yes, sir. I became violent, saying you would regret the day you ever sent me to jail. The guards had to drag me out of the courtroom."

"And your mother was there."

Egan remembered well the look in her eyes that day. For years, he'd felt that shattered expression was because he was going to prison. But it was because he'd been making everything worse with his attitude. Something unfolded inside him, and all the pain he'd been holding suddenly let go, allowing him to see the past differently. Everything he'd done had been in rebellion, triggered by the death of his father.

"I always liked John Rebel. He was a good man, and for the record, I would have done exactly what he did if someone had attempted to shoot my kids. Most people in Horseshoe felt the same way. That's why the grand jury no-billed him." The judge took another drink. "A father should always protect his children. I used to be my daughter's hero, but now she has another hero."

Hollister gulped another drink. "Did she tell you I cheated on her mother? Yep, I did, and there's no way around that. She'll never look at me again the way she did—with stars in her eyes because I was her daddy, the man who could do no wrong." A credit card lay on the desk and he pushed it toward Egan. "That's her credit card. She told me she doesn't need it anymore and that she can support herself. My baby is in New York alone and I don't know if she's hungry or needs anything, because I know she will never call me. So, Mr. Rebel, if you want me to suffer, you're too late. I'm already suffering."

Egan got to his feet and took the glass out of the judge's hand.

"Hey…"

"You've had enough," Egan told him in a steely voice. "Go upstairs, take a shower, shave and call your daughter. Tell her you're sorry and tell her you love her. That's all it takes. Then ask if she's okay and if she needs anything. She will respond in kind. I know Rachel that well. Stop feeling sorry for yourself and stand up and take control of your life again. That's what I'm going to do, Judge."

The older man stood on wobbly legs. "No one tells me what to do in my own home."

Egan took a step closer to the desk. "If you want your

daughter to respect you again, you'll do as I'm telling you. Or you will lose her forever. Your choice, sir." He turned toward the door.

"Mr. Rebel." The judge's voice stopped him.

"Thank you for saving my daughter's life. Twice."

Egan tipped his hat. "You're welcome." He walked out of the house and into the bright sunshine, feeling free for the first time in fourteen years. Really free.

He headed toward Rebel Ranch and his mind was as clear as it had ever been. It was time to live again, and sleep in a bed instead of on the cold hard ground. He'd done his penance, and on this day when he'd faced his past, he forgave himself.

Now, he was going to have lunch with his family, and tonight he would sleep in his bed on sheets that still held the scent of Rachel. And he would think about her and wonder if there was any hope for them. Probably not. He had nothing to offer her. He was a broke cowboy, living on the family ranch. Rachel was used to the finer things in life and he couldn't offer her that. Besides, she was in New York and he was here in Horseshoe.

He would probably never see Rachel Hollister again, but he would remember her for the rest of his life. They'd shared a moment out of time—never to be forgotten.

Chapter Sixteen

Rachel settled into her old life with ease, except for the broken heart. There was no way around that, but the kids in school made life bearable. It was nearing the end of term and everyone was excited. Their last art project was an original work that would account for half their semester grade. She had so many talented children with a keen eye for darks and lights and colors. Some were painting still lifes, some were doing portraits and others, landscapes. Each had a unique talent she found it a joy to nurture.

Rachel and her roommate had always been good friends, and they got along really well until Della's boyfriend began to spend nights at their apartment. It was a two-bedroom, one-bath apartment, and having an extra person afoot was becoming crowded. But Rachel didn't want to tell her to move, because then she wouldn't be able to afford the rent. It was a no-win situation. She kept hoping the boyfriend would find his own place. He lived with his parents in Brooklyn and normally commuted. It was much easier to stay with Della and not face the long subway ride.

There was never enough food in the apartment because Neil ate everything. On her way home from work Rachel stopped to pick up a few groceries for herself.

Della and Neil were going out. On her way to pay for yogurt and salad fixings, she spied a display of SpaghettiOs. Unable to resist, she walked over and picked up a can, thoughts of Egan filling her mind. Oddly enough, that day at the cabin when they'd sat on the stoop seemed like one of the happiest memories of her life. Because she'd been with Egan. Any place on earth was good as long as she was with him. Now wasn't that a sad thought? They were thousands of miles away from each other, but he was in her heart and always would be.

She bought the SpaghettiOs just because...

She had a quiet evening alone and that really got to her. In this big city, with its millions of people, she'd never felt more *alone* in her life. New York wasn't the same anymore. Egan wasn't here.

Her dad called and they had a nice conversation. He said he was sorry and that he loved her. It brought tears to her eyes and she realized she missed being home. She missed Egan.

About one in the morning she heard noises coming from Della's room. Loud, amorous noises, and it irritated her. She had to talk to Della. The next morning as she dressed for work she stared at the can of SpaghettiOs on her desk. There was only one place she wanted to be and she was tired of trying to make things work here in New York when she was lonely. She had two more days of school and she would be free to do what she wanted.

Della was making coffee when Rachel entered the kitchen. "Could we talk for a minute?" she asked.

Her roommate brushed back her long dark tangled hair. "I've been meaning to ask you the same thing." She worked in fashion and her life was busy, hectic and colorful.

"It's about the apartment," Rachel added.

Della swung around from the counter. "That's what I wanted to talk to you about."

"I've decided to return to my hometown. I know we have a lease for six more months." Rachel glanced toward Della's closed bedroom door. "I was hoping Neil would…"

"Oh, Rachel." Her friend hugged her. "Things are getting a little crowded here and we were thinking about moving. But if you're leaving, we'll stay. It's wonderful. I don't know where we'd find an apartment like this we could afford, on such short notice."

They hugged again and Della ran to tell Neil.

By the end of the week Rachel had made life-changing decisions. She resigned her post at the school. She called Hardy and asked if she could stay in the house until she found a place to live. That was important to her. She had to be on her own and not underfoot with his family or her father. She knew they loved her, but they deserved their own life, too.

It was mid-June when she hugged Della and said goodbye to the big city. It was a bittersweet moment. There was a lot she loved about New York, but she was really a small-town girl. Hardy picked her up at the airport and she went home—for good this time. Right or wrong, she'd made the decision.

Monday morning she met with the superintendent of Horseshoe schools for an interview for a teaching job. She knew her name would weigh a lot in her favor, but she was a good teacher and her credentials should stand for themselves. The next day the superintendent called and said she had the job of art teacher for grades six through twelve. She celebrated with her family. Her dad was even there, and though their relationship was strained, they were getting along, and that's what counted.

As Wyatt had predicted, Izzy was sentenced to a state mental facility. Rachel had no argument with that. The man was mentally unbalanced, but she was sure his recent actions had escalated the Rebel-McCray feud.

She had about two months to spend with Erin and the baby until school started, and she was going to enjoy every minute. They swam in the pool and she chaperoned Erin and her friends and played with the baby. He had grown so much since she'd been gone. Rachel was happy, except for one thing. Egan had not made one move to see her. She wasn't quite sure why she'd expected he would, since he'd made it plain they had no future.

She would give him time before she made her move. One reason—okay, the main reason she'd returned home was because of Egan, and she had to see him one way or another. And she had to live with his response. Maybe that's why it was taking her so long to visit Rebel Ranch.

HAY-BALING SEASON was long and physically draining. The Sanchez family had most of the hay baled, and Egan and his brothers were getting alfalfa bales packed into barns and the coastal stacked in rows along fence lines. Some they would sell, but first they would make sure they had enough to feed their large herd and their horses through the winter.

He was dirty, tired and eager for a shower. At the barn, he parked the tractor with a long flatbed trailer attached, and jumped off. His brothers were also finishing for the day.

"Another day of hauling and we should have it," Falcon said, wiping sweat from his brow with the sleeve of his shirt.

Paxton slapped the dust from his jeans. "Phoenix and I have a rodeo this weekend, so we'll be gone."

Elias lay sprawled on some alfalfa bales, but at Paxton's words he sat up. "You always leave when there's work to be done."

"Shut up, Elias. I don't feel like fighting with you today."

Elias jumped up with his fist in the air, a smile on his face. "When is a Rebel too tired to fight? Come on. I dare you."

They gathered round their crazy brother. On cue from Quincy, they grabbed Elias. Quincy and Paxton had his arms. Falcon, Phoenix and Egan had his legs. They carried him into the corral and dropped him into the water trough, boots, cell phone and all.

Elias sputtered and splashed as the brothers stood around laughing, even Egan. Phoenix pulled off his boots, slipped his own cell phone inside one and then jumped into the water. Jude and Zane rode in from checking the herd. Zane leaped off his horse, removed his boots, climbed the fence and joined his uncles. Craziness ensued. They always found a way to beat the tiredness.

On the way back into the barn, Quincy said, "Did you know Rachel Hollister's back in town?"

An invisible fist slammed into Egan's chest. "N-no. I guess she came home for a visit."

"I had to get license stickers for all our trailers at the courthouse and I went over and visited with Gabe. He mentioned that Rachel was living back at the Hollister house. She's home for good and is going to teach art in the fall at Horseshoe schools."

"I never expected that."

"From the way she was looking at you on the day of the kidnapping, I'd say you have a lot to do with her returning."

"How was she looking at me?"

"Like you were her whole world."

Egan made his way toward the barn door, needing to be alone to think. Why would Rachel come back so soon?

"Hey, I'm talking to you."

Egan looked back at his brother. "What?"

Quincy caught up with him. "What are you gonna do about it?"

"I'm going to the house, take a shower, eat something and crash."

"Your call." Quincy shrugged. "Lately, you've been different."

"How?"

"You've been sleeping in your bed, and I like that you've finally gotten that chip off your shoulder." He patted Egan's back. "See you later." Quincy went back into the barn and Egan noticed Jericho standing to the side, watching him.

"What?"

"I didn't say anything."

"But you're thinking a lot."

Jericho pulled off his dusty hat and scratched his head. "I'm just wondering what you're so afraid of."

Life. He was scared to death of life. He could face a man with a gun, fight killer dogs, but when it came to the man-woman relationship, he was scared out of his mind. He'd screwed up his life once and didn't want to do that again. And he didn't want to hurt Rachel.

When Quincy mentioned her name, Egan's heart had pounded inside his chest like a jackhammer, and the urge to see her was strong. But once again he was holding back, because he wasn't sure he had anything to offer her other than a life of toil and worry.

Egan stared at his friend, saw the marked lines of a rough life on his face and knew his secrets were safe with him. "I feel like I'm going to get my head shoved into a toilet again."

Jericho smiled one of those rare smiles. "I'll be there to pull you out, so go with your gut feeling."

Egan thought about it later as he sat in the living room in his jeans, watching TV. Elias was stretched out on the sofa in his underwear. Quincy was sound asleep in his recliner. As much as Egan loved his brothers, he didn't want to live the rest of his life with them.

Why had Rachel come back?

Toward the end of June, Rachel could stand it no longer. Egan had to have heard she was back, and yet he'd made no move to see her. That should tell her all she needed to know. But…she had to hear that from him. It was a Monday and it took all day to screw up her courage to make the trip to Rebel Ranch.

The place was a lot different in the light of day. Barns and outbuildings seemed to be everywhere on this large ranch. Tractors with long trailers attached were parked at the barn. Trucks were parked to the left. It was late afternoon and evidently everyone was still working. She'd chosen the wrong time to come, but she couldn't turn around now.

She parked near a tractor trailer and got out. A bow-legged elderly gentleman with graying hair, a worn hat and equally worn clothes came out of the barn. He stopped when he saw her.

"Can I help you, ma'am?"

She walked closer to him. "I'm looking for Egan Rebel."

His eyes narrowed. "You don't say."

"Is he here?"

Before he could answer, two cowboys exited the barn.

They were punching each other in the shoulders and horsing around, until they saw her. One walked right up to her with a gleam in his eye.

"Howdy, ma'am. Can I help you?" The word *ma'am* washed over her, but it wasn't the way Egan said it.

"Get away from her," the older gentleman said. "She's here for Egan. Go get him and stop acting like a fool."

The cowboy held out his hand. "I'm Elias."

The other cowboy pushed him out of the way. "He's nobody. I'm Paxton."

Two more cowboys came from the barn, stopping the words on Rachel's lips. "What's going on?" the tallest, most broad shouldered one asked.

"This young girl wants to see Egan," the old gentleman said. "Egan!" he shouted, so loudly Rachel's ears popped.

The broad-shouldered cowboy held out his hand. "I'm Falcon, Ms. Hollister. It's nice to finally meet you."

"Thank you." He said it with so much gallantry she had the urge to fan her face.

"I'm Quincy." The other cowboy also shook her hand. "I'll get Egan."

But Elias and Paxton were already shouting his name and he wasn't making an appearance. Maybe he'd made his escape. Rachel's heart sank.

A woman in a long-sleeved Western shirt, jeans, boots and a straw hat came out of the barn. "Why is everyone hollering? Oh…" She walked over to Rachel. "I'm Kate Rebel."

Rachel was getting claustrophobic from all the Rebels surrounding her, and her voice disappeared. She cleared her throat and then froze as Egan stepped out of the barn, with his dog at his heels.

"Why is everyone shouting my—Rachel!" The shock on his face said it all. He wasn't happy to see her. She wanted to turn around and go home, but she wouldn't admit defeat in front of the Rebel family.

Egan's mom saved the moment. "Eden is bringing pizza for everybody, so get cleaned up and meet me at the house, and let's give Egan some privacy with Ms. Hollister." The woman looked at her. "You're welcome to stay."

"Th-thank you."

Before anyone could move, two more cowboys strolled out of the barn and Rachel recognized them: Phoenix and Jude. Phoenix paused for a moment when he saw her and then walked over and hugged her.

"As I live and breathe, if it isn't Rachel Hollister, the prettiest girl in our class. In the whole school."

Jude nodded. "Nice to see you again."

Rachel wanted to say so many things, but the words were locked in her throat as she kept staring at the stunned look on Egan's face.

"Let's go," Kate said. "And stop acting like you've never seen a pretty girl before. I know y'all have better manners."

"Now, Kate, they're just boys being boys," the old man said, and she glared at him.

"Don't start with me, Abe."

Without another word, Kate Rebel's sons followed her. The old man ambled behind, glancing back a time or two. Rachel was left standing alone with Egan, who was still staring at her as if he'd been turned to stone.

"What are you doing here, Rachel?" he finally asked.

He made no move to come to her, so she had no choice but to walk to him on shaky legs. Tired lines were etched around his eyes and dust coated every inch of his clothes and hat. Clearly, he'd had a long day of work.

"I heard you visited my father."

"Yeah. No big deal." Egan's voice was not welcoming.

She bit her lip for patience. "It is a big deal, Egan. You carried a lot of resentment and hatred for a long time, and if you've let it go, it's a wonderful thing. I don't know why you're acting so offended. Am I not allowed to come here to see you?"

"No, of course not."

"Then why are you acting like you don't want to see me?"

"Because I don't."

Rachel felt the words like a blow to her chest. But she gritted her teeth and refused to let them hurt her in the way he had intended. Something was wrong and she had to find out what it was. This wasn't her Egan.

She glanced toward the house, to where two of his brothers were sitting on the back stoop. "Could we talk somewhere more private?"

Egan went into the barn and she followed him. She jumped back, startled, as she spotted a tall, scary-looking man just inside the door. "Oh."

"This is Jericho." Egan introduced his friend.

Rachel held out her hand. "It's nice to meet you. Egan has spoken very highly of you."

The man shook her hand with a strength that was just as startling. "Egan's the best friend I've ever had." After saying that, he moseyed out of the barn.

Rachel stared after him, but quickly brought her thoughts back to Egan. The pungent scent of alfalfa greeted her and there was a lot more hay in the barn than there had been before. He sat down on a fresh bale and rested his elbows on his knees. Pete curled up beside him.

"My father said you had a good visit."

Egan rubbed his hands together. "Yes. I got a lot of the resentment out of my system and learned some things about myself. Mostly, I learned everything that happened to me was my fault. And no one else's."

"How wonderful, Egan, that you're able to admit it."

"It's not so wonderful when you look back and realize you've caused your mother more suffering than she needed at the time."

Feeling brave, Rachel sat beside him. "I'm sure she understood."

"Yeah. That's my mom."

There was silence for a moment and Rachel searched for words, but the ones she wanted to say he might not want to hear. She had to say them, though. "I've returned to Horseshoe for good. I want to watch Erin and Trey grow, and spend time with them. This is my home and I want to live here. I'm looking for a place to rent. Mrs. Hornsby rents a room and I'm going to look at it tomorrow, for starters."

Egan didn't say anything, so she decided to be completely honest, as he'd always been. "If you're thinking I came back because of you, you'd be right."

He looked at her, his dark eyes troubled. "Why would you do that? You and I have no future."

She took a deep breath, his words hurting in a way she couldn't disguise. "Why? My father's not an issue anymore, so tell me why we can't at least date and get to know each other better."

"It's complicated."

"No, it isn't. It's really very simple. I love you. I know that in my heart and I knew it the moment I first looked into your dark eyes. I knew it for certain the night we made love. I don't understand why you can't admit you love me, too. We've known each other only a short time, but sometimes, I'm told, love happens like that. I'm willing to take a chance on us. Why are you so afraid to do that?"

"This conversation is over." He stood abruptly and headed for the door

"Don't you dare walk out on me, Egan Rebel. You at least owe me an explanation. And I demand it."

He swung around, the hurt in his eyes undeniable. "You want the truth, Rachel? I live and work here on this ranch. It's hard work and I make very little money, but this is my life, and someday a part of this ranch will be mine. You're used to the finer things in life and I can't offer you that. Is that simple enough for you? You don't fit into my world. Can you see yourself married to a man who toils fourteen hours a day without rest? Can you see yourself married to a cowboy?"

She stood up. "Yes. If that cowboy is you."

"That's just a fantasy in your head, like it was when we were at the cabin. You can't live in a fantasy world, Rachel."

"You keep putting up these excuses like barbed-wire fences to keep me out. I'm asking you once again, what are you so afraid of?"

He looked down at the ground and didn't answer, and she knew he was never going to give them a chance. This was it and she had to have the courage to admit Egan was never going to love her the way she loved him.

She walked past him toward the door.

"I'm scared of failing." His voice was low, but she caught it. She turned back with hope in her heart. "I screwed up my life so much and I don't want to screw up yours. You deserve the very best of everything and I can't give you that. Please, don't make this hard on us."

She moved to within a few inches of him. "I've been all over the world with my mom and shopped in the most exclusive stores, but I've never been more happy than when I was with you at the cabin."

"You can't mean that."

"I do. It wasn't about where I was. It was about who I was with, and the peace and harmony that filled me just being there with you. That's what it's all about, Egan. That feeling of being complete when you're with that person, and that's the way I feel." She cocked her head to look at him. "How do you feel about me? That's the main question."

He raised his eyes to hers. "I think about you all the time. I couldn't sleep in my bed because the scent of you was there. I kept telling myself I'd forget you, but every day I remembered you more and more. I…I love you. I don't want to, but I do."

It seemed as if she'd waited forever for him to say that, and a tear trickled down her cheek. He wiped it away with his thumb and she leaned her face into the palm of his hand. "Will you marry me, Rachel Hollister?"

Tears sparkled in her eyes. "Marriage? I was hoping for a date."

"I'm in this for the long haul."

Her heart raced so fast she could barely speak. "Then say it the right way."

A smile split his face. "Will you marry me, ma'am?"

"Yes." She threw her arms around his neck and he clasped her tight against him. They held on to each other, enjoying this moment when they'd finally gotten through all the bad stuff. Then his lips met hers and the world spun away, with just the two of them standing against all the forces that had brought them here to this moment.

He kissed her cheeks, her neck and lower. "Where are we going to live?" he whispered against her skin. "I share a house with two brothers and I can't ask you to live there."

She ran her fingers through his hair, knocking his hat to the ground. "We'll figure it out. As long as we're together we can make this work."

He held her face in his hands. "Are you ready to be a cowboy's wife?"

"I'm ready to be your wife."

"I love you, ma'am."

Epilogue

They were married at the end of July in a small church Rachel had attended as a child. A church wedding was important to both of them. Rachel wore a beautiful white gown her father had bought, because it was something he knew Rachel's mother would've wanted.

When she came down the aisle to him, Egan was struck by how much he loved Rachel, and he'd never realized until that moment just how much a part of him she had become. He was now a firm believer in love at first sight. He would love Rachel forever.

Judge Hollister gave a reception at his house and later Egan and Rachel drove back to the ranch, changed clothes, loaded the ranger and headed for the cabin. It was where Rachel wanted to spend their honeymoon. He didn't try to dissuade her, because it seemed important to her.

It was the peak of summertime with no air-conditioning, but they didn't notice the heat. They swam in the creek, pulled the mattress onto the porch and slept out there. Everything was primitive, even their need for each other. They stayed until their food supply ran out, and then they returned to civilization, suntanned and happy.

Egan had taken Rachel to see the Fitzwater place and she loved the old antebellum house as much as he did.

Even the caved-in roof, the buzzards living inside, the rotted boards and the trash strewn around didn't change her mind.

He'd bought a used one-bedroom mobile home and set it up not far from the house. Every day after cowboying he worked on the house, and his brothers helped. It was going to take a while to restore the place, and in the meantime they lived in the trailer. It was small but they didn't care. They were with each other, and Rachel was right. It was all they needed.

Egan and Jericho finished installing the last window late one afternoon.

"That's it," Rico said. "They look damn good."

Egan wiped his hands on his jeans. "Yeah."

A car honked and he turned to see Rachel crossing the cattle guard in her white Mustang. She was now teaching and the days were long without her. He found himself watching the time on his phone so he could quit work when she got home.

"The wife is home," Jericho said. "And I have to get back to the ranch. What's next on the house?"

"Insulation."

"Call if you need me."

Rachel drove up, got out and hugged Jericho. Then she walked toward Egan in her slim-fitting dress and heels. She removed the clip and shook her head until her tousled hair floated around her like a cloud, then paused at the bottom of the steps.

"Hello, cowboy."

He tipped his hat. "Howdy, ma'am."

She squealed and ran up the steps into his arms. He held her for a moment and then kissed her deeply, just to make up for the hours they'd been apart.

Pete barked incessantly at their feet, forcing them to notice him.

"You know what he wants," Egan said.

"I'm spoiling this dog." Rachel bent to hug Pete and then ran back to her car. Pete jumped up and down, eager to see what she had for him. In the yard, she placed two *kolache* on a brown paper bag and he gobbled them up, wagging his tail.

Egan sat on the stoop, watching his wife and wondering why he ever thought she wouldn't fit into his world. She drove the tractor while he loaded hay onto it, and she got up at dawn to go with him to check the herd. She was perfect in every way, and every day she reminded him just how perfect she was in everything she did.

She slipped onto his lap. "The windows look wonderful."

"They turned out really good."

"Were you able to set up a payment plan?"

"No. I paid for them." At her wide-eyed expression, he added, "I used the signed blank check your father gave us for a wedding gift. My mom gave us the house and the land, and my brothers have helped. Even Jericho has given us something for the house. I didn't think it was fair to leave the judge out. After all, he is your father. It just took me a little while to get used to the blank check."

Rachel kissed the tip of Egan's nose and rested her head in the crook of his neck. "I'm so happy. It will bring us closer together and I like that."

"Mmm. I paid for the insulation, too."

She laughed, and he loved it when she did that. He held her just a little tighter.

Pete barked and they looked up to see his mother's truck coming across the cattle guard.

Kate was big on giving them their privacy, so Egan

had to wonder what had prompted a visit. She got out and walked towards them with a picnic basket in her hand.

"I made a big supper and brought some for the two of you. I know how hard both of you are working." She gazed up at the house. "Everything is looking really nice."

Egan stood and took the basket from her. "Thank you, and thanks for letting me get off early every night to work on the house."

She touched his face and for a moment he remembered all the times as a kid when she'd done that, especially when she was proud of him. There had been very few of those days in his teens and college years.

"I'm so happy you found someone, my son, to fill the empty places in you. It's always been my greatest wish."

"I'm sorry for the years I caused you so much pain."

Rachel moved closer to him and Egan slid an arm around her for support.

Kate shook her head. "Just be happy, Egan." She hugged Rachel. "Thank you for loving my son." She walked back to her truck as Egan and Rachel stared after her.

Rachel wrapped an arm around his waist. "That was nice. I like your mother."

"She has a lot of responsibility on her shoulders, and being wild boys, her sons have sometimes made it worse."

Rachel reached up and kissed Egan's cheek. "But not anymore. At least not my cowboy."

"Because of you." He pulled her to him. "Have I told you today how much you mean to me?"

She moved out of his arms toward the trailer. "No, but I'm going to our love nest to get out of these clothes, and you can show me just how much." She took off running.

He picked up the picnic basket and ran after her. "Rachel Rebel, you will never get away from me."

"That's my plan," she shouted back.

Laughter filled the lazy summer afternoon and Egan was happy, really happy, for the first time since his father had passed away. He would never take that for granted again. Rachel had said she'd wanted a forever love, and his purpose in life now was to make sure that happened every day.

"I love you, Egan," Rachel said, standing just inside the doorway in a pink thong and a lacy bra.

All thought left him. He removed his hat and sailed it toward the small sofa, feeling like the luckiest man on earth. "Sweet lady, I love you, too."

* * * * *

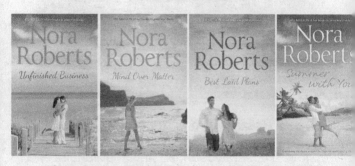

MILLS & BOON®

The Chatsfield Collection!

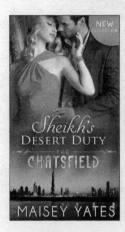

MILLS & BOON®

Cherish™

EXPERIENCE THE ULTIMATE RUSH OF FALLING IN LOVE

A sneak peek at next month's titles...

In stores from 17th April 2015:

- **The Pregnancy Secret** – Cara Colter
  and **Not Quite Married** – Christine Rimmer

- **A Bride for the Runaway Groom** – Scarlet Wilson
  and **My Fair Fortune** – Nancy Robards Thompson

In stores from 1st May 2015:

- **A Forever Kind of Family** – Brenda Harlen
  and **Bound by a Baby Bump** – Ellie Darkins

- **The Wedding Planner and the CEO** – Alison Robert
  and **From Best Friend to Bride** – Jules Bennett

0415/23

Join our *EXCLUSIVE* eBook club

FROM JUST £1.99 A MONTH!

Never miss a book again with our hassle-free eBook subscription.

★ Pick how many titles you want from each series with our flexible subscription

★ Your titles are delivered to your device on the first of every month

★ Zero risk, zero obligation!

There really is nothing standing in the way of you and your favourite books!

Start your eBook subscription today at www.millsandboon.co.uk/subscribe